Pronoti Datta was a journalist for over thirteen years, covering culture and society in Bombay. This is her first novel and she draws much inspiration from the city. She lives in Bombay (minus cats or children) and works as an editor of digital content.

Half-Blood

Pronoti Datta

SPEAKING TIGER BOOKS LLP
125-A, Ground Floor, Shahpur Jat
New Delhi—110049

First published in India by Speaking Tiger Books 2022

ISBN: 978-93-5447-025-7
eISBN: 978-93-5447-033-2

10 9 8 7 6 5 4 3 2 1

Typeset in Garamond Premier Pro by SÜRYA, New Delhi
Printed at Chaman Enterprises, New Delhi

For Pranab, Rati and Sarosh

PROLOGUE

Dear Moonie,

I call you Moonie because your mother wanted to name you Mahtab, which in Persian means the moon. It's a beautiful name but too heavy for a little baby. So I prefer to use my pet name.

I hope you're a strong, smart girl when you read this letter. I know Mini will raise you well, she's a lovely person, the only one I could entrust with your care. She would have been able to bring you up in a way I couldn't have. I'm deeply sorry to have left you Moonie, but I hope you will trust me when I say that it was the best thing I could have done. And I hope you will forgive me.

You see Moonie, I did a terrible thing for which I had to leave Bombay. I don't want to burden you, in this letter, with the details of my deed—or my life. It's a long story and I'm not a man of words. The choice is yours. You might not want to know any more about me, which I understand completely. But if you do, then these are the people who will tell you about the circumstances that forced me to leave Bombay and about my background. I give below their names, addresses and numbers (for those who have telephones). They know that you may, one day, get in touch with them.

Homi Sukhadia
Arsiwala Chawl, Room 11, ES Patanwala Road, near Rani Baug, Byculla.

Hilla and Jimmy Kapadia
Naval Baug, Block F, Flat 405, Lalbaug, Parel. Tel: 4710122.

Imelda Braganza
Sunshine, Second Floor, Dr Cawasji Hormusji Street, Dhobi Talao.

I don't have much to give you Moonie except my love and these few objects I have enclosed in this box that are special to me. Be well, study hard and stay happy.

With love,
Burjor.

1

The Petit Sanatorium, a sandy bulk on Warden Road, always seemed to me stranded on a shoal of the past. The early twentieth century building, solid, masculine with a few floral flourishes, appeared to occupy a separate dimension that shared borders with the rest of the area. It was empty, windows either broken or boarded, and the ground was patrolled by a single watchman, who stood at the gate looking out on the main road with the resignation of a man doing time. The building had once housed Parsi couples with no permanent homes. I imagined if you entered, you'd find a pack of forgotten, feral Parsis stinking of sweat and despair, periodically loping up to the cracked windows to glimpse daylight. Had Burjor lived here?

Outside, a Parsi man and woman had made the pavement their home. They sat corralled by their things, rolls of bedding, a pile of trunks covered with tarp and a couple of mutts they'd adopted. I'd come to interview them for they were the only homeless Parsis in the city—and to take a closer look at the sanatorium, which was pictured on a postcard I had. He was sour-looking with crooked teeth and a hunch. She was a slight figure with a simian face, sloping shoulders and long arms that barely moved as she walked. The woman was nuts about dogs. I'd seen her feed and pet every stray on her way back from the public loo under the Kemps Corner flyover. The only time I'd seen her smile was when she was scratching some dog's ears. The rest of the time she sat glumly on a plastic chair or fought with the man who may or may not have been her partner. Ordinarily a story like this would be a front-page anchor at the paper where I worked. Zoroastrians, an increasingly rare species, easily made headlines. Two homeless ones in a community considered rich was unheard of. But they appeared to be fibbing, contradicting each other, and a trustee of the sanatorium, who I'd spoken to earlier, said they'd been evicted some years ago and refused to leave the pavement despite being offered a decent sum. He said they were distant relatives, she denied his claim. Whom to believe? There was no story in it for me.

Down the same pavement, koli women sold cheap fish. The scraps fed a family of uncommonly healthy cats. One grey and white male unfurled himself near my feet and moseyed off in the direction of his lunch. Had Burjor known his great-great-grandfather?

I began walking towards the Kemps Corner junction to hail a cab, past the street's other ancient edifices: Sunama House, whose entrance has the fetor of raw chicken from the cold storage on the ground floor, and Banoo Mansion, capped by a giant masonry crown.

The cab was a cross between an altar and a strip club. A rosary dangled from the rear-view mirror and magnets with images of Mary and Jesus on the cross, decorated the dashboard. The ceiling had two large mirrors set in a carpet of red felt. A metallic pole bridged the gap between the front seat and the roof of the cab. A sticker of a pair of inviting, kohl-lined eyes gazed at me from the rear-view mirror. The upholstery might once have been taupe. Now it was stained deep brown in patches, no doubt by all the perspiration that had seeped into it. The cabbie spoke English.

"Bleddy hot no?" he said, in a Goan accent. Streams of sweat coursed down his neck, into his collar and percolated into the aquifer of his upholstery.

"Ya."

"It's July and there's no rain, bhenchod."

"Ya."

"You're married or what?"

"No."

"Why you're waiting, madam? When I was your age I had two-two children. You're how old?"

"Thirty-four."

"Your time is passing, madam."

He wasn't entirely off the mark. I too felt time slipping from my grasp. But not biological time. The sight of babies was yet to stir my womb. It was more an existential time. The nagging knowledge I'd drifted through life doing nothing worthwhile in thirty-four years. I'd tried plenty of hobbies looking for that one meaningful vocation. Old-fashioned ones like pottery, philately, gardening. New-fangled ones like origami, rolling sushi, cheese making, Buddhist chanting. I briefly took to storytelling, joining a group that met once a month to tell each other personal stories. Finding the meaning of life on a dentist's chair, falling in love on Facebook, overcoming gluttony, seeing cosmic messages in billboards. It was cathartic for some—they couldn't help tearing up. The audience teared up too and it all ended in a group hug. My tales were all made up since I had no stories worth telling. None of the activities lasted. Then I began looking for Burjor.

"Tell your mummy-papa to find you a nice boy, OK?" the cabbie said.

"OK."

I don't mind chatter from kooky strangers. It's amusing and supplies me with stories that I can later tell. Sometimes I'm accosted by aging men at the club, who spend their days shuffling between the lounge and the bar, making boastful conversation. The last masculine strut before old age shrinks their bodies and adds a quiver to their voices. I was particularly receptive to taxi drivers as Burjor had been one. Even in the seventies, when there were more Parsis working blue-collar jobs, a Parsi cab driver would've stuck out. He was uncommon enough to be profiled in a newspaper, probably a journalist who'd been a passenger. The story was titled: 'Weird wonder: Bombay's bava cabbie'. The persistent love for silly alliteration. Journalists had grown moronic over the years but the headlines they wrote were as terrible back then. Would Burjor startle passengers with conversation like the perspiring Goan cabbie?

It was four o' clock by the time I entered the newsroom, a huge hall illuminated by blazing tubelights. It was just starting to get lively. Reporters were coming in from the field. Though some had no doubt come from home, after having had lunch, perhaps a nap. Their stories of the day might have been texted to them by a journalist friend from another newspaper. Beat reporters across papers shared details of routine stories. This meant that even if one couldn't make it to a press conference, the site of a collapsed building or a slum demolition, one could still file the story. If you're in the habit of reading papers closely, you'd have noticed that the language of stories on the same incident are often suspiciously similar. Purnendu Purukayastha, the excitable city editor, was striding around when I walked in.

"Ay Maya, khabar acche?" Do you have any food?

"Na."

"Shala..."

Purnendu, foul-mouthed and always greedy for food, darted off towards a reporter dangling a bag of chips. He reached into the bag with a clumsy, forceful motion and crammed a fistful of wafers into his mouth glistening with the unctuous sheen of junk food. He was fondly called Boomba, a pet name he shared with the actor Prosenjit. Boomba was tallish, skinny with a disproportionately large head and slightly protuberant eyes shaded by a thick awning of eyelashes. They gave his face a feminine youthfulness at odds with the incipient sag of age at the corners of his mouth. He affected the aggressive machismo of a parar dada, a neighbourhood bully, scattering abuse like birdseed as he scurried down the aisles of the newsroom. The man had a group of favourites, all men, all Bengali. As I settled down at my desk, I heard him scolding one of his sycophants, a particularly odious civic reporter called Shomshuddho Nag.

"Shon bana, aajke shattar aage story na dile, tor beechi kete phelbo." Listen you dick, if you don't hand in your story by seven, I'll cut your balls off.

Boomba was one of the few entertainments of a job as dull as it was comfortable. I was an editor on the desk, which meant that every day I had to read opening lines like: Forget about the living, there's no peace even for the dead (Trustees of an Andheri cemetery were found trying to sell the plot to a builder). The underworld strikes yet again (A builder was shot at by an assassin in Ghatkopar). If you thought of going to Goa for New Year, think again (High fuel prices had bumped up domestic airfares).

Like most things in my life so far, a career in news was something I'd gone along with. Mini had got me an internship after college and, finding myself without significant passions that could lead to other careers, I'd stayed on. Even college had been Mini's doing. She'd studied in Calcutta and taught English at Wilson College, where even students from the city's good schools spoke a street-level lingo. The Bombay slang I grew up speaking, an argot of Hindi, English, Gujarati and Marathi that I now fetishized as nostalgia, infuriated her. So Mini, with her low opinion of education in Bombay, decided I would study in Delhi, in a college that had a reputation for turning out bureaucrats and politicians.

I studied Philosophy, a subject that, again, Mini suggested I take up. She felt it suited my contemplative personality.

"I think you're mistaking a lack of things to say for thoughtfulness," I'd said.

"Don't sell yourself short," she said, with the eternal optimism of parents.

In college, I'd been greatly taken by the idea of an authentic life. To do something with utmost conviction, to remain unyielding before the forces of people, the economy, whatever was trying to bend you to its will, to be uncompromising. Stories of people who'd persisted in their beliefs, fielding scorn and disapprobation, and emerged victorious, moved me. Gandhi, the tree-hugging Sunderlal Bahuguna, Medha Patkar, Souza. My friend Ameya, who rejected the path drawn by his parents for him—he could either go to IIT and become an engineer or to IIM to study finance—to become a puppeteer. Though his light was dimmed when I learned he'd made the choice after inheriting a sum so vast from a deceased grandparent that, if they wanted, even his grandkids could afford to be puppeteers.

The idea came from my dishy professor Gaurav Tripathi, who taught a class on the German and French existentialists. It was hard not to be swept by anything he said as he paced up and down the small classroom in a beat-up green corduroy jacket with leather elbow patches, Naga print scarf and the aura of a one-time hippie. Watching him chug Navy Cuts, drawing deeply on the cigarette from the corner of his mouth, holding the smoke for a breath and then exhaling expertly, was mesmeric. He drove to college in a jangling black Ambassador. While discussing Camus's *The Myth of Sisyphus*, he gave the example of his car.

"The Ambassador is my Sisyphean boulder," Tripathi said. "No matter how many parts I change, how often I get it serviced, it breaks down every few months. It's futile but I'm tied to the car. You guys think it's a rattling cage and wonder why I bother with it. But being inside, sitting on the worn, leather seat, breathing in a decades-old scent, is reassuring, womb-like."

All of us in class were seduced, even though we knew the truth. Tripathi had a bigger, more baffling weakness. For all his intelligence, he was a sucker for ponzy schemes. He'd put money into several get-rich-quick programmes and, being at the tail end of the pyramid in each case, he'd been one of the losers. His savings were rock-bottom, he lived from paycheque to paycheque. He couldn't afford a better car. But the illusion only added to his charm.

Tripathi, while discussing authenticity, explained that we're spurred to create meaning in our lives by the knowledge that our lives are meaningless. The idea presents itself in the form of death, an occurrence both inevitable and shocking. If life is to end anyway, what's the point of it all? The point is to make lived experience amount to something, Tripathi said, by making choices that are true to oneself. Once again, he offered himself as an example. "I could've been an IAS officer with a secure job and government housing," he said. "That's what my parents wanted for me. But I chose to teach because I felt this country needs good teachers more than it does administrators." The truth was he'd failed the IAS exam on three occasions.

We were told this by Dr. Kaul, who taught us about the ancient Greeks. Kaul took pleasure in poking fun at his colleagues, especially Tripathi, salting our classes with gossip. He introduced us to Socrates, who may or may not have dropped the pearl, "Know thyself". The authentic life was one of self-knowledge, Kaul explained. "Now look at my friend Tripathi," he said. "He's been married three times. Each wife walked out on him because he cheated on her. He claims he strayed because they'd drifted apart for other reasons but the fact of the matter is he can't help himself. He's not made for monogamy. He needs to see this, stop chasing after a missus number four and save himself and her a lot of pain." Who was he chasing? Kaul didn't say, realizing he'd said too much.

My classmates could not have known how deep those two words had struck. Could you know yourself without knowing your past? Look where it got Oedipus. For years, I'd felt stymied by the mystery over my origins, relying on others to make decisions for me. Of course, a part of my paralysis was laziness and fear of what I might discover if I gathered the will to investigate my foundation, to stand at the ledge of my abyss and peer into its depths. "It takes balls to confront your reality," Kaul said, while discussing Kierkegaard, whose thoughts on dread revealed my own feelings with shocking clarity. "Let me give you a cheap example. If my friend Tripathi had the courage to look inside himself, he'd see that his skirt-chasing stems from a fear of loneliness. If he recognized this and learnt to be alone, he'd be doing himself a favour." We later learnt why Kaul repeatedly mocked his colleague. Tripathi had made a move on his wife.

What I wanted above all was to write. My singular passion was reading, it was the only thing to which I truly applied myself. And I wanted to be able to produce words the way the writers I admired did. But the words had to come from some spring of experience, they couldn't emerge from the yawning hole I was reluctant to plumb. What words did come were of no use. The Hole didn't stop me from having visions of greatness.

Bellow's Herzog wrote imaginary letters to people. I had imaginary interviews with journalists about my first novel, a wild success. The interviews were always self-deprecating as if to compensate for my own conceit.

I can't bear to read the book now. It's so embarrassing. Take my advice, don't read it.

I'm surprised it won any awards. If I was on the jury, I wouldn't pick my book. Now I know how that sounds, I saw your eye-roll. I'm not saying I'm not thrilled. Let's just say I wish I'd written a better book.

"What you're thinking, Maya?"

"Nothing man. You're looking kind of thakela."

"I'm fucking consti. I haven't crapped in three days."

Meera Chatterjee, also known as Tumpa. An old school mate and one of the few Bengalis I'd known as a kid growing up in Bombay. Back then most kids in class belonged to the city's old communities—Gujaratis, Bohris, Parsis, Marwaris, Catholics, Maharashtrians. Pale with hair like a bushel of wheat framing an equine face and thick eyebrows she plucked and tended as if they were bonsai, Tumpa looked Persian. But she was as scatological as a Bong raised in Behala.

"Shit ya. Isabgol? Or have some prunes. They lubricate your system like nothing else. It'll just glide out."

"I tried Isabgol. Didn't work. And I had three prunes this morning. Nothing. Not even a pellet."

"Try beetroot. Boiled. It's fail-safe. Just don't turn to look afterwards. Your potty will be red."

"I'll try it. If it doesn't work, I'm going to OD on a cocktail of laxatives. Dulcolax, EvaQ, Laxayu."

"Sounds killer man."

"I'm despo dude."

We spoke a mutilated language we'd learnt as kids, horrifying the Bongs from Bengal and Delhi, who had no equivalent, no dirty middle English. What drew us Bengalis together was talk of shit. Like a low frequency hum only we could hear, it pulled us from across the newsroom. Soon we'd be swapping faecal anecdotes about consistencies, remedies, frequency, idiosyncrasies. Tumpa's chronic constipation was well known. Purnendu had the opposite problem, an irritable bowel. "Salad khele shesh," he'd say. Salad kills me. And Shomshuddho, his bootlicking minion, stayed away from coffee and papaya as they jammed his system.

Tumpa had come to look over my shoulder as I edited a story she'd written on an outcome of 26/11. She'd interviewed a few of the victims recovering in hospital and their devastated families. In the months after the attack, we carried pages full of stories on survivor accounts, the ongoing investigation, intelligence failures. I was particularly attentive to these stories as 26/11 had considerably disrupted my life.

We noticed a huddle at one end of the newsroom and left the desk to investigate. A group of reporters and editors were standing around Daniel Chacko, the bureau chief, hunched over something. As soon as he walked off, they closed in. The lion had fed, now it was the turn of the scavengers. The sound of fingers being sucked and murmurs of satisfaction could be heard. Purnendu was at the centre, hoovering a paper plate piled with food. Kebabs and pao had been ordered from a joint at Crawford Market and various people had laid out a buffet of dabbas of homemade lunch. I threaded my way into the mob to snag the final kebab. Purnendu, who must have had several by then, reached for it at the same time. Upper lip lacquered with grease, he said, "Bhaalo meye, chhere de." You're a good girl, leave it.

"Na."

"Chol, fifty-fifty."

"Remember the piece I did about the guy who was shot during the firing at VT but survived?" Tumpa said as we walked back to my seat. "Can you believe the way Boomba edited that story? He made my opening sentence, 'A bullet got Bilal, a factory worker from Khopoli, down but not out. The feisty 27-year-old displayed Mumbai's spirit of resilience by bouncing back'."

"Like he's a tennis ball or something."

"I open the papers in the morning to find my story massacred," she said. "Either it's chopped badly so it makes no sense or it's been filled with clichés or been given a shit headline. Did you notice the headline for my piece on how well Taj's staff handled the crisis? 'Guests rave about Taj's bravehearts'. A rhyming headline."

"That might have been Chacko. He has a thing for rhymes."

"I'm shit scared to read the papers knowing that some or the other embarrassment is waiting for me. And the day I expect something like that to happen, I crap badly. My bowels go on strike."

"You've got discerning bowels."

2

As I said, the attack made a pretty drastic impression on my life. I nearly lost two significant people, Shivaji, who I'd known all my life, and Homi, who I was yet to know. In fact, it would've been surprising had 26/11 occurred without knocking me off my feet. You see, in the past, major events in the city's history had coincided with revelations about my life. If I believed in fate, in teleology (a clunky word that handsome professor Gaurav Tripathi uttered with such attractive fluency), I would have believed in the romantic idea that my fate was intertwined with that of Bombay's. While discussing Wittgenstein's theory that many philosophical problems could be pinned down to the way we used language, Tripathi would bring up the idea of luck. "I would never wish you good luck," he'd say, smoking sexily in Delhi's winter fog. "I might say, for example, 'I hope you ace your test', but I'll never say 'best of luck'. Because there's no such thing. You can see how casual usage of the term suggests there is something like luck or destiny, a guiding hand that determines the course of life." Reading philosophy threw that juju out the window. There was no fate, only chance.

Yet, thinking about the historic coincidences produced a feeling of meaning and strangeness. From the beginning, I'd felt untethered from the world, like a balloon adrift. The sense was brought about by the fact that I resembled no one in my family, physically or in character. Shivaji and Mini are short, the colour of malt and round-cheeked like a lot of Bengalis. Shivaji is chubby all over. Mini has cartoonish curves, big breasts, a narrow waist, a generous ass. I'm tallish, absurdly fair with a lanky, boyish body. No breasts or hips, bony shoulders, hair as straight as my pin-like frame. There was not a gesture, habit or trait we had in common. When I was introduced as their daughter, people couldn't help showing surprise. We'd learned to ignore the looks but as a kid in school, it was hard to avoid the speculation. Kids, unschooled in tact, wouldn't hesitate to ask questions like, "Maya, how come you don't look like your mummy-daddy?" I was afraid to know why and so I lived with the feeling of being authorless, like the Vedas, I liked to think. I was appositely named too. Maya, meaning compassion, but also the web of apparitions that constitutes the world.

When I did get answers, the timing was significant. Every piece of self-knowledge was accompanied by a major event in Bombay. For every convulsion in my life was a parallel upheaval in the history of the city. As a result, I felt tied to Bombay and developed an interest in local history. I read books, took long walks in old neighbourhoods. Often I'd have Kersi for company. Kersi, a yoga teacher, lives a couple of floors below me in the building in which I've grown up. We were occasional lovers and he supplied me with weed.

Now Kersi was a real character, a person of extremes, what they call a mad Parsi. As a teenager he kept a rat snake that had to be let loose in Borivali national park after it escaped into his neighbour's house. He collected 'found objects' long before they began appearing in art works in galleries, filling drawers with neatly labelled zip-lock bags containing things like discarded rubber chappals, stamps, lost keys, torn pages from books. He called his collection the Museum of Randomness or the Museum of Lost Stories. "Better you call it museum of kachra, rubbish," his mother would say.

At some point in his twenties, Kersi fell hard for his neighbour's daughter Aarti Punjabi, the one who'd found his rat snake curled in a corner of her living room. But she wasn't interested and when she married her college sweetheart, Kersi, heartbroken, burnt her name on his forearm with a lighter. He would unburden himself to me from time to time on the terrace of our building where he'd go to smoke and I'd go to do jumping jacks and skip with my rope. I was ten years younger and discrete for my age. When I met Aarti in the lift or at her place when her mum invited me for koki, the stiff Sindhi breakfast paratha I adored, she'd tell me about the ways Kersi stalked her.

Kersi took to yoga after years of a sedentary chartered accountancy job, which busted his back. He applied himself with the same intensity with which he attached himself to everything else, practicing every day for years. Once he mastered the scorpion pose, he quit teaching. Not long ago, Kersi dated a Bengali girl fifteen years younger than him. She walked into his class with her apple-shaped face, almond-shaped eyes she lined with kohl even at seven in the morning and a red vest that exposed a tattoo on her back, the word 'bidrohi'. She told him it's Bengali for 'rebel' and that she'd had it tattooed during her years as a politically active student at JNU. Only phonies do things like that, I told him. But Kersi, reading her as a kindred spirit of extreme passions, asked her out the following class. Besotted, Kersi was eager to know sentences like 'I want a kiss' in Bengali. (He supplied me with free weed in exchange for Bengali lessons.) I tried to explain that there's nothing seductive about 'aami chumu khabo'. She dumped him after a few months claiming things were getting too "intense". Then one day, as Kersi and I smoked companionably in his room, which had long been emptied of the Museum of Randomness in a raid by his mother, he leaned over and kissed me.

"What is this? Rebound?" I said.

"No, I've always been curious," he said.

We ended up in bed. Yoga had made his body sinewy, youthful. Next to him, I was acutely aware of my thin, undefined frame. He smelt of smoke and light sweat, an odour I found so stirring I buried my nose in his armpit for long minutes.

"What a weirdo."

"Look who's talking," I said, my voice muffled by hair and skin.

We'd walk around Kala Ghoda, the art deco stretch by Oval Maidan, the grid-like streets of Fort, the skinny lanes of Dhobi Talao and the avenues of Ballard Estate. The last walk was our favourite. We'd start after a lunch of pulao at Britannia or beer, cheese balls and unruly club sandwiches at Cafe Universal and walk slowly, looking up at the windows and balconies. Each time, we'd spot something new. For instance, on our third walk around the area, we chanced upon a terrific Bombay Port Trust insignia on a building gate on Calicut Street, a round plaque with four circular frames with painted images of a lighthouse, ships and the mainland. I'd amuse Kersi by turning on my tour guide voice.

"Ballard Estate was designed by the architect George Wittet in the early twentieth century in the Edwardian style. You'll notice the buildings are simpler than their predecessors, the city's neo-Gothic edifices. There's less embellishment, the buildings are square, business-like. And this here is the Karfule petrol pump, built in the art deco style and run by the Sequeira family since 1938. See the tower on the roof? It used to have a clock."

If the day was pleasant, we'd wrap up Ballard Estate,

cut across PM Road and the Cross Maidan thoroughfare and walk down the art deco flank of Oval Maidan.

"These buildings came up in the 1930s around the time land was being reclaimed in a big way to meet the city's housing needs. You've heard of the Backbay Reclamation Scheme. Art deco was in vogue in Europe and the city's well-travelled folk brought the style here. Many of these buildings were designed by local architects, most notably GB Mhatre, who also designed the Karfule petrol pump we saw earlier today."

"Enough, masterji."

"Some of the most common decorative elements found in art deco buildings are the ziggurat, radiating lines, geometric patterns. Look at Rajjab Mahal, a glorious example of the style. Notice the sunburst, the zigzag motif, the design on the glass panel in the middle. Another fine example is Empress Court here. Look at the curved balconies. Many art deco buildings have these locomotive-shaped verandahs."

"You're reminding me of an old school teacher all the boys found hot," Kersi said. "I'm getting hard listening to you."

"You're bored, I get it. Let's have coffee."

The solid bulk of these buildings had a reassuring effect. Terrestrial, weighed by material and history, they felt like anchors tethering me to the reality of the city. That's why I never tired of walking the same streets. Neighbourhoods with stone buildings like Fort and Ballard Estate were particularly salubrious. The stone, mined in Malad, in Porbandar, looked indestructible, capable of withstanding the harshest elements, giving me a sense of place. Because of my interest in local history, I was offered an occasional column in the paper. I'd written about Bombay's water fountains, street names, colonial milestones, most which were half buried in layers of concrete, statues, urban villages and forgotten landmarks. It earned me a degree of respect at work, placing me above the average desk editor.

3

I entered the lives of Mini and Shivaji Deb in 1975. It was the year of the Emergency. Mini, who ran with a left-leaning crowd of teachers, artists and social workers and had an interest in politics, was electrified by the upheaval and the talk in those circles. She came from a family of Marxists. An uncle and a cousin had been active in the Naxal movement, taking bullets and doing time in jail. Her parents' place in Calcutta had no framed pictures of gods, only photos of Lenin and Trotsky. How had they married her to this man?

Shivaji, on the other hand, an entirely apolitical animal, was unperturbed. It pleased him that a result of the autocratic manoeuvre was that the trains ran on time. Naturally, they fought. Mini contemptuous of Shivaji's apathy, Shivaji telling her that people were entitled to their opinions. Those days, they argued even if there were no solid reasons to fight. It was into this atmosphere thrumming with hostility that I entered, a wailing squall.

Mini, with her dramatic eyes and attractively droopy

mouth, looks like she has a big personality. One can imagine her as a lively director of Tagore dance dramas or a sociable gallerist. In fact, the opposite is true. Mini is quiet, made to suffer. And she *was* made to suffer by Shivaji and our maid Ratna. Her name was Ratna, but she was no gem. Ratna from Rakhalgachhi was thin, gaunt with cruel eyes, a flair for drama and a voice that could drive a person to self-harm. She was loud, even when she was soft. With that level of natural amplification, Ratna could make herself heard over vast spaces. When she argued, which was often, we had to shut our ears. After years of tolerating Ratna, Mini's nerves were wafer thin. With Mini she was mutinous, never following instructions, doing the opposite of what she was told. But with Shivaji, she was a lamb. She was there to stay because Shivaji loved her cooking. Her paatla machher jhol, kumro bonti and chingri bhapa were more precious to him than Mini's happiness.

Shivaji had never really grown up. He'd been indulged as a kid as only sons are and he was indulged as an adult. As a young brat, he would throw tantrums if the beguni wasn't crisp enough and a fresh batch would be made. He would, like all devious Bengali kids, threaten to fast every time his father refused to hike his pocket money. His mother would intervene and Shivaji would get a raise. When the maid complained that the teenaged Shivaji would brush against her and pretend it was accidental, his parents accused her of lying and fired her. Shivaji denied it of course. He was their shona, their moni, their shonamoni, their Tublu raja.

Mini had never understood the Bengali fondness for Maratha names. They weren't martial like the Marathas, who'd wrested parts of Bengal in the eighteenth century and should, for that reason, be hated. Shivaji was short, unfit and he came from a family of overweight people. Yet, several in the Deb family were named after Marathas. There was an uncle fondly called Bappa after Bapparao, another one was called Tanaji, a couple of distant cousins were also Shivaji.

They first met at Mohuapishi's house in Calcutta. It was an arranged set-up. Shivaji was a fleshy twenty-five-year-old in a bush shirt and bell-bottoms that were too tight. The knolls of his man-breasts made forks in his shirt. When he walked, Mini noticed, the tops of his thighs rubbed against each other. Why did Mini, who was beautiful, smart and capable of quoting Shakespeare, marry this blob? In hindsight, she told me, she was appalled at herself for finding him attractive. But to her twenty-four-year-old eyes, there was something endearing about his studious, chubby face. She liked the thought of his substantial bulk weighing her down in bed. Most of all she liked the fact that his job as a chartered accountant would soon take him—and her—to Bombay, far from the oppressive embrace of family.

Mini had imagined in Bombay they could live as a modern nuclear family. They would both work—he at the company that had hired him, she at a college—and come home in the evenings, exhausted but happy. There would be no one to look out for but each other. No in-laws with dietary habits that had to be indulged. Shivaji's mother ate meat and fish only on Wednesdays, Fridays and Sundays; his father ate meat and fish all days of the week but hated tomatoes and leafy vegetables. Then there were the things that made them flatulent. Cauliflower and tuvar daal made her fart; he got gassy on legumes. That left them with potatoes, all the mucilaginous veggies and pumpkin, which both Debs could eat in any form—fried, stir-fried, curried. But they liked it best as a ghonto, sickly sweet and cooked to a pulp. There would be no prying pishis, pishos, kakus, kakis, jethus, jethis dropping in unannounced for tea and jalkhabar, which would mean making something elaborate like Moghlai paratha or samosas or chops. Mini hated to cook.

But Shivaji was equal to all of them. He was a diva to beat all divas. He wanted Mini home before he got home so she could be ready with tea and jalkhabar. Biscuits wouldn't too. The snack had to be substantial, Calcutta style. If the vegetables weren't cut right, he'd throw a fit. For chorchori, veggies had to be cut dumu-dumu, in fat chunks. But for shukto, he liked them kuchi-kuchi, diced small. Mini, who didn't care, often got it wrong. Then there was fried fish. He liked his moch-mocha, deep-fried till it was reddish and crisp on the outside. Mini's fish was never moch-mocha enough. Growing up, I'd often hear versions of this argument.

"I must have fried that fish for fifteen minutes at least," Mini would plead.

"Obviously it wasn't enough. How many times do I have to tell you it's no fun eating maachh bhaja if it's not moch-mocha."

"I'll get it right next time."

"Before we got married, your parents told mine your cooking was excellent. They lied."

"Don't eat the fish, have the rajma. Tell me how it is."

"I don't eat rajma. It gives me gas."

After some years of swallowing his tantrums, Mini started giving it back. Usually she'd attack his weight.

"You're a fat hangla," she'd say. "Look at your thighs."

"You're no Twiggy yourself," he'd say.

But she did exactly what Shivaji wanted. The impulse of wifely devotion was too strong. She'd seen her mother and aunts suffer demanding husbands, and they'd made too deep an impression. Of course, Shivaji knew this and used it to his advantage. He'd been an ace at manipulating people since he was a kid.

It was true about Shivaji's weight. The chubbiness that Mini had once found attractive soon became grotesque. His neck was thick and ribbed, his torso was a rapid of flesh, his expansive belly wobbled like freshly set caramel custard.

Sex became a problem. As Mini's confidante, I was privy to things I didn't care to know about. When she needed to unburden herself, which was often, I had no choice but to listen. Bearing the load of a man who was nearly a hundred kilos of adiposity was no joke. All that fleshy kneading greased by the film of sweat between their bodies, Shivaji's shallow breathing, his tendency to look everywhere else but her put her off sex. Luckily he never lasted long—his weight had robbed him of stamina. It might have been alright had Shivaji been an adventurous lover. Mini was, in her head at least. She'd have liked him to try different positions, go down on her once in a while, pin her down and make forceful love. But he rarely went south of her collarbone. Because sex embarrassed Shivaji. He had a strangely Catholic approach to it.

"Sometimes I used to think he must be a gay," she said.

"Gay," I said.

"A gay, yes."

"Just 'gay'."

They moved to Bombay in the early 1970s and rented a small two-bed near Colaba market. It wasn't far from Ballard Estate where Shivaji worked in a company that made ball bearings. The business was owned by a Marwari family called Agarwal. As is the case with many family-run businesses, Shivaji's boss, a large man who wore two-carat diamond baguettes in his ears, treated his employees like valets. Even if they happened to be managers like Shivaji. Mr Agarwal, who unbeknown to his strictly vegetarian family ate meat outside the house, had on several occasions asked Shivaji to hop across the road to Britannia to get him a mutton berry pulao and caramel custard. He also shouted at his employees and called them names in full view of the office just to put them in their place. Shivaji took all of this with great equanimity, showing a capacity for humiliation at odds with his personality at home.

"At home you are an ustaad, in front of that mota Marwari you're like a mouse. Why don't you grow some ball bearings and get another job?" Mini would say.

The boss's family had a share in one of Bombay's textile mills and Shivaji had listened to Mr Agarwal rant for years about mutinous labourers. In 1982, when I was seven, the strike to beat all previous strikes, the one that ended the textile industry in the city took place. It was to be the last for the mill; they were going to shut it down. Shivaji, who displayed a sly subservience at work, defended his boss even at home.

"Your capitalist bosses have grown fat on the backs of these workers. Have you even seen how they live?"

"You're a fake Leftist. You enjoy the perks of my job yet you complain."

"You talk like you're doing me a favour. I pay for stuff too, run the house, look after Maya. You barely acknowledge she exists. Now don't say she wasn't your idea!"

Since it's a small house, I was always within earshot. On that particular day, I was right there in the living room, reading my book of Russian folk tales for the tenth time. I got a real kick out of the stories of Baba Yaga and her hut that stood on chicken feet. The one good thing about having parents from Cal was that they knew books. No *Mr Men* for me; I was started off on illustrated Shakespeare. By the time I was fourteen, I'd been through the Complete Works, read most of Austen, Maugham, Orwell, Hemingway and Virginia Woolf. Daphne du Maurier was considered light reading at home.

"What did you mean when you said 'don't say she wasn't your idea'?" I asked Mini later.

After thinking for some time, Mini told me I was adopted.

4

My parents were Parsi, a couple known to her, Mini said. They'd been unable to care for me for reasons she didn't go into. Relief! Joy! Finally, I knew why I resembled no one in my family. Thank god, for the Debs were generally loathsome. What a pleasure to know there was no blood between me and my odious cousins in Calcutta! (Mini's side of the family didn't bother me; it was small and full of adults.) Those over-achieving brats with whom Shivaji never failed to compare me. Montu, who at the age of eight was showing signs of a career as a concert pianist; Bhombol, who wasn't far from becoming a chess grandmaster; Rani, who had at the age of ten exhibited her paintings in a gallery, a series of mother and child works clearly similar in style to Jamini Roy, whose prints were all over her house. There was also fear. What had made my real parents give me up? Were they alive or dead? Would they one day return to take me away from Mini? To be snatched away from this chubby creature redolent of Eau de Cologne, who'd spoken to me as an adult for as long as

I could remember, indulged me, introduced me to great literature... The thought was unbearable and I decided immediately not to ask any questions or repeat the one Mini hadn't really answered. What had she meant by "don't say she wasn't your idea"? Mini said she would tell me more when I was old enough to understand and that suited me fine.

Mini had a word with my teachers in school. I knew by their bright smiles and sudden affection. Naturally, word spread and for a brief period, my classmates treated me as someone special, a godly incarnation in their midst, a child with a supernatural gift. Unused to attention, I was unnerved—and pleased. When the class bully taunted me—"Maya, your parents didn't want you or what?"—my friends retaliated, "Just shut up, you stupid!"

Naturally, as an adult I followed the mill lands issue with interest. When I crossed Lower Parel, past the malls and apartment blocks that glinted like crystals in the sun, past the rubble of mill structures that would be cleared to lay the foundations of high-rises, I felt joined to the city's history. Later, when I learned Burjor had lived for years in the mill district of Lalbaug and secured jobs for people as textile workers, I would experience this bond more keenly.

I could lay no claim to the Zoroastrian tradition—the flight from Persia cradling sacred fires, assimilating into the alien culture while holding on with (foolish) doggedness to the old country by the thread of blood, throwing up giants in every sphere of public life. In Parsi restaurants, I felt the strangeness of my situation. The food should have been familiar in an everyday way yet it was exotic. On the other hand, I was too removed from the Bengali centres of Calcutta and Delhi to feel Bengali. I didn't know the songs my cousins and Purnendu sang or their street-level vocabulary. Instead I felt like a daughter of Bombay moulded by its great upheavals. Sometimes on Sunday mornings, Kersi and I would walk around the Lalbaug area, taking in the derelict mills behind locked gates and the chawl-like buildings that housed former mill workers, before winding up at Ladoo Samrat for a deep-fried snack. On those walks, I felt a pleasant gravitational tug, a cord tying me to the earth.

Once Mini told me I was adopted, I instinctively knew that I was Mini's idea and that somehow Shivaji resented her for it, and that I was the taper kindling their daily spoken and silent feuds. Till then I'd assumed their fights arose from a general incompatibility, Shivaji's food habits—and Ratna.

Shivaji sprang Ratna on Mini one Sunday. It was a cruel surprise. He pretended he needed a haircut and when he returned, Ratna was with him. She'd arrived at VT on the Bombay Mail from Calcutta, wrapped in a cheap, polyester sari, her oiled hair in a severe bun, her lips stained orange from chewing paan. Shivaji's mother had poached Ratna from a friend's home and dispatched her to Bombay. Her daughter-in-law was no good at being a wife. Her son needed a vegetable or a fritter, a daal, a fish or meat curry and rice every day. Mini cooked like a novice and when she was tired, she made sandwiches. Sandwiches! How was her son to sleep if he didn't get rice! Ratna had been briefed in Calcutta. She was to take orders from Calcutta on the dinner menu and how to run the house and she would gather intelligence on Mini, where she went, the kind of friends she had, what time she came home. So when Ratna arrived, she had the look of a conquistador. Seeing her superior gaze and Shivaji's guilty eyes, Mini knew she didn't stand a chance.

In Ratna, Shivaji found a comrade for she was as xenophobic as him. Finally, another Bengali in this cosmopolitan building! Mini had tried to change him with art and people. She'd drag him to galleries in the hope that art would open his mind. But he got bored. She'd have her bohemian friends over for dinner so he could see what he was and what he was missing. But he thought they were degenerate and phony. It was always "those bloody Gujjus" or "that demented bava" or "that Punjabi has zero class". He sought Bengalis out like a hungry dog nosing for scraps. That's how he joined a group that organized an annual Durga puja, enthusiastically taking on dull administrative responsibilities.

Mini, who'd never been a fighter, didn't have the stamina to sustain a protest. She argued with Shivaji for some days before giving in. And picked a few fights with Ratna before realizing she was up against a gladiator. Because to fight with Ratna for the smallest thing—could she use less oil while cooking, did she have to make a racket while washing the steel dishes, why was she so rude to the bai who cleaned the house—meant starting her off on an angry tirade that could last hours. She had a real athletic voice; once it got warmed up, Ratna could rail tirelessly. It didn't matter if Mini shut the kitchen door and locked herself in her room. Ratna went on till she was spent. It was always the same outburst, starting with how much she did and how little she was appreciated, segueing to her impoverished childhood in Rakhalgachhi, her father squandering their land to pay for his debts, moving to Calcutta to do what was once unthinkable for a high caste family—work in people's homes—losing all hope of marriage because she had to work and send money to her parents, losing all hope of having a child, the one thing in the world she most wanted. The only times Mini felt a pang of affection for Ratna was when she'd utter a piece of village wisdom. When peacocks cry, it means the rains are coming. If a lizard calls out three times in a row, someone is remembering you. Whistling at night attracts cockroaches.

Mini and Ratna had one common ground: me. I arrived at the Debs' not long after Ratna. She loved me from the moment Mini entered the house with my swaddled frame in her arms. Shivaji, her other love, behaved like a stranger. He issued no fatherly hugs, no tender cuddles, no childish gibberish. At the most, he'd scratch my head when I scored well in a test. Not that I minded. Ratna and Mini swamped me with hugs and kisses and fought with each other over how I should be raised. Ratna liked braiding my hair in two tight plaits. But Mini thought the hairdo looked provincial. Mini wanted me to eat healthy. But when she was away at work, Ratna fed me tasty, fatty things. Mini took me to the park and let me loose to run around and play with other kids while she read a book or strolled. Ratna, on the other hand, kept a vigilant eye and issued a stream of instructions—don't run too fast or you'll trip and scratch your knees, don't get on the slide your pants will get muddy, leave that dog alone it's filthy. When it came to education, Mini gave me books, showed me movies, took me to art galleries. Unlike most parents, she didn't bother with my homework, didn't care when I did poorly in a test. "You won't learn a damn thing in school," she said. True but I had to work with what I was given. Shouldn't Mini have taken some interest in my studies? Pulled me up for bad test scores, asked what I was reading in class? She was deliberately laidback to impress me—which kid wouldn't want a hands-off mother—and make a point to Ratna.

Appalled by Mini's laissez-faire attitude, Ratna was a strict minder. She pushed me to study every evening, quizzed me on multiplication tables, made sure I stuck to the study schedule tacked to my soft-board when it was exam time. She soaked almonds for me because they were good for memory, forced castor oil down my throat to lubricate my bowels, made me do breathing exercises.

There *is* such a thing as too much love. I knew all about it. By the time I finished school, I felt wrecked by the mothering impulses of Ratna and Mini. How had I made it through school with a sound mind? In college in Delhi, away from the competitive affections of Ratna and Mini, and comforted by the effects of weed, which was available on campus in abundance, I felt calm for the first time in years. Gradually Ratna's battering voice, which I'd carried as a ringing sensation in my ears, a Bengali tinnitus, receded.

—

We lived across Strand Cinema, in a four-storey. On the same floor lived a Jewish family, the Samuels, and the D'Mellos, a Catholic couple. There were four Parsi couples, a couple of Gujarati families, three more Catholic families, two Khoja families, three Sindhis and Makarand Bhandarkar, an ageing anglophile Maharashtrian bachelor who walked around wearing a sola topi. For all his affectations, he bought Bal Thackeray's sons-of-the-soil rhetoric. He got kicks out of telling Shivaji whenever they met by the lift that he was no Maratha warrior. "All you Bangalis are useless except for Subhash Bose. He was a fighter. The rest of you are pansies." By the time I reached my twenties, the Catholic families had sold off and gone to Borivili and Vasai and three out of the four Parsi couples had passed away, childless.

Old man Bhandarkar died at eighty-five. I was ten at the time. He was returning from his morning walk and, as usual, he bumped into Shivaji on his way to work. "Ay Chhatrapati Shivaji, I can smell your mustard oil in my house. Dirty bloody stink. You don't have a sense of smell or what? All you Bangalis think you're damn clever eating all that fish. Your brain might be big but your nose is blocked." A second later he clutched his chest, buckled and fell on Shivaji.

Since Bhandarkar had fought with his relatives, none of them showed up to cremate his body. Turned out he didn't have many friends either. Mini and Shivaji did what had to be done. Shivaji kept the sola topi and took to wearing it on his evening walks, a gesture that prompted in me a rare feeling of affection for the guy.

Back then people often kept their doors open and walked in and out of each other's homes. When you travelled up the lift, you could smell what each family was cooking—vinegary Goan curries, beef stew, biryani, mutton dhansak on Sundays, dried bombil, fried bombil, the powerful miasma of sea fish. And suddenly on the third floor, the sharp scent of mustard. Most of the Catholics left once their families grew too big for the small apartments and moved to the western suburbs. By then people had stopped leaving their doors open, otherwise the smell of coconut oil would have drifted down the lift shaft, for a Malyali family moved in when I was in my twenties.

Sometimes the Katraks and the D'Mellos would send over bowls of prawn patia and pomfret moile. Mini and I would eat all of it since Shivaji couldn't stand the smell of sea fish. He only ate river fish, rohu, katla, tilapia. Getting pork or beef home was out of the question. When we wanted some, we'd go down the street to New Martin for a plate of Goa sausage and pao. Or to Yolande D'Mello, our Catholic neighbour, who came over whenever she had to make and answer phone calls.

The Debs, the Parsis, one Gujarati family and Bhandarkar were the only people with phones in the building back in the eighties. So two out of five doorbells a day usually meant a neighbour wanting to make a phone call. Shouts for neighbours to come answer their calls echoed along the building corridors all day long. This way everyone knew what was going on in everyone else's lives. For instance, Mini knew that Mrs D'Mello suspected her Julius of cheating on her with that slut Maria from Mazagaon, who he'd met at a card game at his good-for-nothing friend Godfrey Figureido's house. Sometimes Maria called for Julius and if Yolande answered, she pretended to be a colleague. Mini could see why Julius D'Mello had lost interest in his wife. She'd seen pictures of Yolande as a young woman, slim with a neat bob and bangs wearing knee-length dresses that skimmed her figure. After ten years of marriage, she was barrel-shaped with thick ankles and a neck like a tree trunk. The weight didn't bother her. This was part of life, you got married, had kids, got fat. She wore floral dresses with scalloped necklines and high waists that drew attention to her substantial stomach. Overall, she looked sturdy, capable of weathering through the shit life threw at her and emerging intact like a flowery Rock of Gibraltar. Maria didn't stand a chance.

To return the favour, Yolande would feed Mini—meatloaf, potato chops, vindaloo, prawn pulao—and listen to her complain about Shivaji. "Why don't you have a baby?" Yolande advised. "It might make Shivaji less khadoos. I'll pray to Jesus to give you a child."

5

The first time I left Bombay was to go to college in Delhi. Late that year, 1992, and in the early part of 1993, Hindus rioted against Muslims. And in March, a series of thirteen retaliatory bombs were set off across the city. Away in Delhi, I feared for Muslim friends. My childhood friend Aliya barely left her flat in Bombay Central—Muslim homes were sacked down the road from where she lived. The men in her building kept vigil on the terrace for approaching mobs and all the families kept their curtains drawn for days as if to make the building invisible. They all bought knives. Later Aliya learnt they weren't seriously at risk. A neighbour had gang connections. One word to the don and he'd send his foot soldiers.

Aliya's relatives in Bhendi Bazaar lived close to Suleiman Usman bakery, whose attendants were fired upon by cops. They saw men being hacked and their bodies tossed into drains. One of Mini's friends, a psychoanalyst, went looking for mobsters, wanting to figure out what drove them. He met a group of men at Nagpada, freshly high from a day of mayhem and asked how they could bring themselves to kill their own neighbours. They said Muslims deserved to be wiped out. So he handed them his card and told them to call when they needed a shrink, when they stopped sleeping and had nightmares of those they'd slaughtered. They called him names and shooed him away. Three months later, one of the guys showed up at his home. He was being haunted by a woman he'd stabbed. She followed him from room to room, rode the bus with him to work, watched him while he tried to sleep.

Meanwhile in Delhi, I was getting a lesson in comparative religion of a different kind. On the second day of college, I was stopped by Aditi Sharma, a senior.

"What caste are you?" she said.

"I don't know," I said. If she'd grabbed my ass, I'd have been equally shocked.

"Amazing, she doesn't know what caste she is. Find out!"

That evening, I called Mini from the phone booth in campus to ask.

"There's some confusion in that department. We thought the Debs were kayasth. Though your grandmother would like to think you guys are boddhi because some grand-uncle decided he was boddhi and started wearing the thread. If I were you, I'd go with kayasth. There's more cache in being non-Brahmin."

"What the hell is a boddhi?"

The issue was debated last year after Shivaji's father

died. My grandmother wanted the shradh, the ritual death ceremony, to be held eleven days after his passing like the brahmins and boddhis, who are a rung below, do. But the priest would have none of it. He insisted the Debs were kayasth and that we'd have to do the shradh after thirteen days. I had somehow missed the controversy. But I remember thirteen painful days of eating vegetarian food without onion and garlic in Calcutta. And the rank smell of my grandmother's scalp. As part of the mourning ritual, she used no soap or shampoo for two weeks. Her head reeked of stale sweat and grease and little nondescript things clung to her hair. When Mini and I got desperate, we'd go to her atheist parents' place to eat or to Park Street for mutton-egg rolls.

"So?" said Aditi Sharma, the next time I ran into her.

"Why do you care?"

It was a habit, an instinctive classification of people by surname and community. "Sharma—brahmin, Rathi—jat, Singh—could be sardar, jat, Rajput, bhumihar, Yadav depending on where the person is from, Nair—nearly brahmin. Welcome to the real world," she said.

I began doing the same thing involuntarily, matching names to communities. Maria Joseph—Syrian Christian. Arun Jha—brahmin from Bihar. Anamika Mathur—kayasth from the north. Peter Renthlei—Mizo. It was a learning game for I was meeting people from all over for the first time. Some of them, you couldn't tell what they were by their names. I lived with two of them in a flat in Vijay Nagar, not far from college. Mohua Das, a Bengali Christian. A Bengali Christian! I hadn't come across one since Michael Madhusudan Dutt, whose poems we read in school. She wasn't Catholic when it came to men though, playing two guys at the same time, one in Delhi, one in Calcutta. The other, Priti Singh, was Rajput Christian. She held Bible readings in her room, a spartan affair dominated by a picture of her amaranthine love, Jesus, on the wall. Sometimes I'd walk past her door to see a group of girls caught up in the liturgy, their eyes wet, fingers gripping their books. Priti, normally an unsmiling, sepulchral figure, would be in a state of intense animation as she read and sermonized like a bob-haired Moses.

Bombay was provincial compared to this. The corridor at college was like a scene from the great migration. Herds of boys loped down the Serengeti of the hallway at any time of day. The jats, bulky with solid chests and heavy faces, most of them in one sporting team or another. The boys from Mayo, mostly rangy, fine-featured Rajputs with archetypal looks suggesting a tight gene pool. Malayalis, sleek, compact of body and spectacular on days they decided en masse to wear white shirts and mundus. The north-easterners, stoic, stylishly accoutred, sauntering down the corridor with shoulders slightly hunched, even the short ones. The posture gave them an aloof air, a mien suggesting they'd descended from a superior habitat.

The Bengalis were more heterogeneous and rarely moved around in large packs. There were the pot-smoking, Doors-listening, Tolkien-reading guys from Calcutta's classy schools. Friendship was eased if you spoke Elven tongue. There were boys from Calcutta's more modest schools, who ribbed each other in dirty street Bangla and knew the lyrics to both Tagore and salacious songs. And then there were the guys from small towns like Asansol and Medinipur, who in the first few days of term walked around with the diffidence of people returning to society after a long exile.

The girls didn't move around in kindred packs. Except for the north-easterners, who stuck to each other—Mizos with Mizos, Nagas with Nagas—because there was strength in numbers. They were then, as they are now, seen as aliens and easy targets for cheap men. Like the boys, they had an effortless cool, long torsos, thick but firm legs, sheet-like hair, all wrapped in cheap but chic clothes.

In general, girls didn't swagger around the place. There was a sense of being overwhelmed by men, who were in greater number, of being pushed to the margins. This is not to say some didn't stand out. A few girls made quite an impression on me. One of them was Padma, a third-year lit student from Kottayam. She had skin the colour of molasses, which made her eyes appear bright white. She was whippet-lean with a mop of short, untameable hair she cut herself. Aditi Sharma, the girl who'd asked me my caste, contemptuously called her "kaali billi", black cat, behind her back. Padma was the brightest girl I met in college. She talked to herself and made gestures as she walked with quick, short steps. She kept to herself a lot and the few friends she had were the bookish sort who you knew would end up academics. She had an unstudied haughtiness, especially when she was talking with impressive fluency about subjects like Proust and Plato.

I was smitten, so was my classmate Shubhendu, who supplied her with free weed just to be close to her. Once as the three of us smoked on the lawn, Shubhendu tried to impress her with his knowledge of the personal lives of philosophers.

"You know I've been studying the exercise regimes of philosophers and the idea of body-mind fitness," he said. "Look at Kierkegaard, Wittgenstein, Kant. They were fit, lean men. Kierkegaard walked a lot, Wittgenstein was all about manual labour."

"Kant was fat," Padma said, and walked off shattering Shubhendu's chubby heart.

Then there was Shonali, tank-like, sneering and openly gay. Few people liked her for she could be rude and insulting if she thought you weren't worth her time. But since she was something of a math genius, she had the grudging respect of everyone. Boys, who felt threatened by her brain and the aggressive movements of her body, liked to feign being scared of her. And cry that it was such a waste her girlfriend, a gorgeous, vacuous exchange student from the US, was gay. With me, Shonali was like the cool Bengali uncle, who despite his heterodox ways was conventional about certain things. She was always after me to study more, spend less time "doing ganja with your faltu friend Shubhendu or what little brain you have will soon evaporate". She was fond of me perhaps because I was quiet and, like her, an oddball, a Bengali with a Persian face.

"Tui ki jeeneesh?" she'd say. What kind of thing are you?

"*Tui* ki jeeneesh?" I'd say. "Buddhiman aar boka blonde. What a cliché." What are *you*? A brain hooked to a dumb blonde.

—

In the first year of college, I had an education in difference. An amusing instruction on campus and a violent lesson back home. It was the first time we, my friends in Bombay and I, were aware in an active sense about religions, community. Aditi Sharma would've laughed and called me a privileged naif. I was unprepared for Bombay's climate and the stories I heard. Meher, who lived on Breach Candy, a neighbourhood rarely touched by calamity—it doesn't even flood in the monsoon—told me she'd mustered her building pals to come up with a plan to beat back the sword-wielding hordes when they arrived. They stockpiled soda bottles on the terrace that they could rain on the mob and drew up a timetable for lookouts. The terrace was patrolled by pairs in shifts. Muslim families moved into their non-

Muslim neighbours' homes and replaced nameplates on front doors with Hindu names. Naturally, no one showed up and they dropped their vigil. "If they had come na, we would've taken them," Meher said. "We were ready for those chooths man."

A peon in Shivaji's office, Rafique, had had to flee his home in Tulsiwadi. His slum was mobbed in January by a group of Hindus led by a corporator. Some of the men in the mob were Rafique's neighbours. They fire-bombed the Muslim shanties after looting them. Rafique and his family escaped to a relief camp in Madanpura. Shivaji, who rarely went out of his way for humanity, was moved enough to offer Rafique temporary shelter and when he said he could manage on his own, gave the peon money and clothes. Mini joked that his generosity of spirit was thanks to her; even though he tried to shut her out, some of her qualities had rubbed off on him.

I was reluctantly moved. Shivaji, a creature of habit, an entirely predictable animal, had done something surprising. He wasn't a charitable person—he rarely donated money, he complained about beggars and almost never had a good word to say about non-Bengalis. Yet, he'd been willing to let Rafique into his home. The last time he'd done something this uncharacteristic was to organize Bhandarkar's funeral. Of course, he'd taken me in, a fact I tended to forget.

"Shivaji is an inert being. It takes upheavals to get a meaningful reaction out of him," I said to Mini.

"You shouldn't talk like this about your father you

know," she said. Mini would mouth off about Shivaji as much as she pleased but she didn't like others doing the same thing.

"You agree with me."

"Yes, but he's still your dad so you should show some respect."

"No, he's not. Some crackpot bava who gave me up to two demented Bongs is my father."

Mini and I were in the balcony sharing a joint. I was home for the holidays, just a month after the blasts had wrecked the city. Mini had walked in on me enjoying my nightly toke and reaching for the joint, had smoked it like she had experience. We were cloaked in an aromatic mist, buoyed by the mildly euphoric effects of weed. This pleasant state was soon torpedoed by my life's second great revelation.

6

I lost my virginity in college to a boy called Danish Khan. We met during an audition for *Evam Indrajit*. He was directing a Hindi version of the play and was known as something of a rebel among the theatrewallahs. It was a time of intense discovery—we were finding our feet in an unfamiliar terrain of books, theory, people, testing ideological niches to see where we fit. There was a great deal of intellectual jousting. Ideas were commandeered like posts and verbal duels were fought. Danish had broken away from the main theatre group because they only did English drama, which he considered inauthentic and upper class. Why were we speaking a foreign language when we should be talking about things that mattered to us in our own languages? He was one of the few truly bilingual people around, able to read and write fluently in English and Hindi. At the time, he was making his way through the novels and stories of Bhisham Sahni, Manto, Harishankar Parsai and Surendra Verma and was never seen without a Hindi novel in hand. He carried it around like a badge. He also only wore kurtas and made it a point to speak in Hindi in group conversations even when everyone else spoke English. I was a sucker for this sort of intellectual swagger and I fell for him immediately. Later when I described him to Aliya, she said, "He sounds like a choot."

I was a backstage hand in the play. We hardly spoke till a party in a poky flat in Vijay Nagar. *Evam Indrajit* had won a drama competition and we were celebrating. He looked older than twenty-one years and had heavy-lidded eyes and a thick mouth stained the colour of espresso from cigarettes. One of his many boasts was that he'd been smoking from the age of thirteen. That night he wore a black pathan suit and looked so good I couldn't stop myself sneaking glances. Of course he noticed. He was at the centre of the room cloudy with smoke from Navy Cuts and joints, Saturn surrounded by circles of cast and crew, many of them randy girls in cotton saris. At the time, wearing saris was something of a rage among a certain set of artsy girls. The place stank of Old Monk and a vile punch made with vodka that was dirt cheap and as lethal as petrol, the greasy odour of parathas and various bodily vapours. Agastya, a senior in Philosophy, was there. He sat in a corner and read Kant's *Prolegomena*, darting looks at the sari brigade to see if they were checking him out. He'd brought his own gin and tonic, which, he explained to anyone who bothered to ask, had become his drink of choice after reading Graham Greene.

At one point, I stepped outside on the terrace for a break from the noxious atmosphere. We were on the top floor of a three-storey building in a row of similar, squat apartment blocks with balconies like wide grins and peculiar architectural flourishes. This one had scalloped arches. The place I occupied down the road had hacienda-style awnings. I felt a tap on my shoulder. It was Danish. Without a word, he leaned in and kissed me, his mouth wet and smoke-bitter and his body damp with alcoholic sweat. We made out for a long time. I could hear people come out to the terrace, scurry back inside, muted giggles and whispers. It gave me pleasure to think of the sari-wrapped girls reacting with jealous surprise. They'd been flirting with Danish in Hindi all evening. And here he was making out with a girl who spoke a mutilated Bombay-Hindi and dressed like a tomboy.

I'd been kissed once before, by a boy who'd lived in our building in Bombay for a short time. I had the feeling he was trying to replicate what he'd seen in porn films for he had straightaway stuck his tongue into my mouth and pressed hard as if he were trying to reach my tonsil. But I knew this was the real deal as I felt a hot knot of arousal between my legs. We went to my place, which was dark and sauna-humid because of a power cut. The landlord kept his door ajar till he went to bed to keep an eye on our comings and goings and on who would come over. He didn't like boys entering. So we tiptoed past his dark door to my flat, where Mohua and Priti were asleep with their room doors open to let the little breeze from the living room window circulate. In my room, we lit candles and sweating, fell on to my mattress. There was a lot of fumbling and untutored movement. I had no experience and Danish, only a little. When he practically swabbed me with his tongue I wanted to laugh. How ridiculous we must look! Then there was a tearing pain and a gentle lurch as he came in the condom. I reached between my legs, ecstatic to see blood on my fingers. It had been done. I had crossed the Rubicon to experience. We giggled like kids, snuggled and talked all night. In my head, we were already dating. I saw us in the future, living together, getting married in an unfussy ceremony, decorating our home with stuff from handicraft fairs, having sex in our new kitchen.

In the morning, I made him tea and eggs like a girlfriend. Mohua and Priti had been surprised to find him at home. He'd walked into the living room as they lounged on the sofa bra-less in t-shirts and undies. They went away and re-emerged in pajamas, their breasts in shape. Before he left, we kissed for a long time.

At the door, he said in English, "Listen Maya, I want to do this again. But just so there's no weirdness later on, I want to let you know that I'm not ready to date or anything. I want to experience life first. Theek?"

"Yeah, of course," I said. "I feel the same way."

—

As Mini and I smoked companionably on the balcony, I felt eager to take her into my confidence. I marvelled at the rhythm we'd established so quickly, leaning forward to exhale through the balcony grills to keep the smoke out of the house, making sure not to wet the filter, tapping the ash outside the window before passing the joint. The pleasant mood, the elation over smoking weed with a parent was a powerful emetic. I felt I could tell Mini anything and she would understand. It's a dangerous impulse as parents are contrary, inconsistent creatures. A single quirk doesn't mean a liberal outlook.

Mini's silence told me I'd been impulsive in telling her about Danish. She stood for a long time without saying anything. Finally, she turned to me and said, "Is this what we sent you to Delhi for? Instead of studying, you're up to no good."

Why, why had I allowed myself to fall for the deception of the moment?

"I study all the time. This is part of growing up too. I'm sure if you examine the statistics, you'll find that eighteen is way higher than the average age at which girls lose their virginity in India."

"You think you're so smart. What if you'd got pregnant? You're eighteen Maya, a child!"

At that moment, I thought of the little shrine in Mini's room. As a form of rebellion against her Marxist parents, Mini believed in god or, as she liked to put it, "an energy". Her chosen gods were the most hedonistic of the pantheon. Shiva, the great lover, was of course represented by the linga (which Mini had no hesitation calling a phallus). There was Krishna, who made a cosmic art of loving freely and had sixteen thousand wives. There was Kali, her naked, big-breasted torso clad in skulls, and Tara's sinuous topless figure. A little Tibetan bronze sculpture of a bodhisattva locked to his willowy consort in yab yum, an upright clasp so erotic, I couldn't look at it as a pubescent without feeling some heat. Every day Mini sponged this tableau and decorated it with flowers. The shivling was crowned with either periwinkles or a hibiscus.

I remembered also the stories Mini told me from the books she read when I was around fifteen. I was perhaps too young to be told the stories but when Mini got excited by something she read, she had to tell someone. Shivaji wasn't interested in anything literary so that left me. She read out bits from the *Mahabharata*—the king who tried to send his ejaculate to his wife with a stork, the sage who seduced a sixteen-year-old—and the *Shiv Purana*—Shiva's tumescent phallus falling off his body, and, spontaneously aflame, setting fire to half the world. Yet, we'd never had the birds and the bees talk. I'd had to figure it out by myself. I looked up the dictionary but that doesn't tell you what goes where. She told me dirty god stories but threw me out of the room when she wanted to watch *Flashdance*. Parents are strange creatures. At that moment, the contradiction between her fondness for sex-laden myths and her prudish reaction to my confession was lost on her.

"We used protection," I said, but she got angrier.

"You shouldn't be thinking about all this till you finish your MA."

"Maybe you've forgotten what it was like to be young. But at this age, sex tends to be on top of one's mind."

At that, she did what she had never done when I bothered her as a kid—she slapped me hard across my right cheek.

"You're just like your father."

"Shivaji?"

"Burjor."

That was the first time she'd said his name in years. The effect was more stinging than the slap. I was immediately seized by the childhood fear of being snatched away from all that was familiar. Turning on my heel, I fled to my room, locked the door and threw myself into my nightly cave of pillows.

7

The next morning after Shivaji left for work, Mini cornered me.

"We have to talk about how you were adopted," she said. "I brought it up three years ago, if you remember, but you brushed me off."

"Because I didn't want to know. I still don't. I don't care how I was adopted. If this is some kind of revenge over me having sex for the first time, it's cruel."

"I promised Burjor I would tell you. Hear me out and then decide whether you want to investigate."

Burjor and Mini had met in 1974, the year before I was born. He used to drive a cab around Colaba and often dropped Mini to Wilson College in the mornings. He was gregarious, fluent in English and sophisticated for a cab driver. He wore smart clothes, expensive-looking watches.

"He told me he'd started out as a taxi driver and then branched out into other businesses. When we met, he drove the cab for fun, he liked to meet people," Mini said.

"What other businesses?"

"I don't know but I wouldn't have been surprised if it wasn't all above board."

Gradually they became friendly enough to meet after she was done with college. They developed feelings for each other though these remained unexpressed. Their worlds were too far apart; the relationship could exist only in the realms of friendship and fantasy.

"You're telling me you fell for a cab driver?" I said.

"Yes."

"A taxi driver?"

"Yes. That bothers you? This isn't conversation for an eighteen-year-old but let me tell you that everyone has blue-collar fantasies."

Blue-collar fantasies! One day she was scandalized I'd had sex as an adult. The next, she was telling me about sexual desire. Did she not see the contradiction! I was so staggered by what I was hearing, I forgot my own dread.

"Besides he wasn't your average working-class type," Mini went on. "He didn't *look* like a taxi driver, which helped. He was tall, attractive, kind and funny."

"If you tell me you slept with him, I'll throw up."

"What happened to believing in a classless society? You, who hates Ratna, give me hell when I insist she wakes up early on Sundays. 'Why can't she sleep late if we can?' But me finding a taxi driver attractive disgusts you. Do you really believe your own spiel about class or is it a trendy idea you picked up on campus? He was your father. Yet, you haven't questioned me about him even once. I've been waiting for you to ask. But you're a bloody coward."

Burjor might've been a looker. But Mini fell for him because he listened. It was to him she confided her problems with Ratna and Shivaji. She talked to him at length about her husband's limited view of the world, his lack of adventure and his adoration of Ratna. She complained about Ratna, who had made herself indispensable to Shivaji and his parents by cooking things he loved and passing on intelligence on Mini's activities to Calcutta. Her in-laws, who were retired with nothing to do, nourished themselves with vampiric appetite on Ratna's scraps of gossip. For Mini, it was thrilling to have a man-friend with whom she could speak so freely. In fact, she felt liberated enough to hint at her disappointing sex life.

"You don't even talk to your girl friends about your sex life out of wifely duty, yet you unburdened yourself on a stranger."

"Yes, but not in detail. It was one of those freak times in your life when you behave in a mystifying, uncharacteristic manner."

They'd go to Irani cafés for chai and khari or bun maska. Café De La Paix at Opera House was a favourite. If they were hungry, they'd go to Military Café and share a plate of kheema pao. On days they felt indulgent, they'd go to Bombelli's at Churchgate for steak. Mini corrected him when he held the knife in his left hand.

She taught him how to hold a wine glass, to leave his soiled napkin crumpled on the table when he was finished; there was no need to fold it neatly.

"Did Shivaji know? Did he suspect?"

"No. I told him later."

Mini told Burjor she wanted kids but couldn't have any. What she didn't tell him was the problem wasn't with her but Shivaji. She'd put herself through tests and they all indicated a healthy apparatus. So the doctor suggested Shivaji be tested.

"What a fit he threw," Mini said. "He flat out refused. It took me weeks to get him to agree. And sure enough, his sperm count was too low for him to have kids. He didn't speak to me for a month. That didn't bother me but I was mad that he didn't tell his maa and baba. It was too big a blow to his ego. They thought I was 'barren' and he let them believe it."

So did Mini, being a wife in the classical mould. Shivaji's parents gave her a hard time for years, rarely missing an opportunity to drop a nasty barb. Mini suggested they adopt. But he couldn't take the idea of rearing someone else's child. Like most men, Shivaji, who wasn't exactly a prime specimen, had faith in his seed. To be let down by his own body was shattering.

"He said what if the kid has a genetic abnormality or grows up to be stupid or ugly."

No wonder Shivaji was a reluctant father early on. We spoke to exchange information and the only affection he showed me was a weak hug on my birthday.

On days I pleased him by scoring well in class tests, he'd buy me things I liked to eat like sev puri, vada pao, Frooti, packets of jeera goli, leaving them on the dining table for me to find. But on the whole, he was a silent presence, wrapped up in his own misery over how life in Bombay had turned out for him. The times I saw joy on his face was when he discussed old Bengali movies with Ratna—the chemistry between Uttam Kumar and Suchitra Sen, Runa Laila's voice—and ate a satisfying meal.

Perhaps he might've warmed up had I shown an interest in Rabindrasangeet or learned to read Bengali, so I might one day inherit the family's substantial collection of Bangla literature, which he never read but was proud of nevertheless. I made a half-assed attempt at singing when I was in school. I made Mini sign me up for Rabindrasangeet classes. Once a year, the woman who ran the classes directed her students in a Tagore dance-drama at which half the city's Bengalis showed up. One of the few moments Shivaji felt real pride in me was when I was chosen to be part of the chorus for one of the dramas. I was dolled up in a sari, flowers and five layers of make-up. After the show, Shivaji and Mini came backstage.

"Great show, Maya," Shivaji said, beaming.

Mini was dismissive. She thought dance-dramas were silly and hated seeing kids with painted faces.

"You look like a clown and the show was a joke," she said.

"Mini!" Shivaji was outraged.

My tryst with Rabindrasangeet was short-lived. A visiting cousin left me a mixed tape of rock. It had The Stones, Dylan, Springsteen, Rush, the Ramones. The music took a grip on me like moss on a wet stone and I couldn't listen to anything else. Tagore's sweet, sad melodies went out of the window.

"Before I pass out with curiosity, tell me what happened between the two of you," I said.

"What would happen? It's not like I was going to leave Shivaji, as tempting as the thought was at the time. I didn't have the balls. Obviously, you don't have the same problem if you could, you know, get together with that boy at this age. I don't think Burjor was seriously interested either. He was seeing your mother at the time."

"Incredible, both of you cheating on your partners. What do you know of my mother?"

"Not much except that she was a seamstress. She stitched Burjor's trousers. You have his face but her colouring. I know this from his description of her. But I'll come to her later."

It's hard to describe the feelings that were leaping through me like atoms in motion. I had recently read Sartre in college and I remembered Antoine Roquentin standing before the roots of a chestnut tree, nauseous. Mini's words had given rise to a knot of nervous tension in the pit of my stomach that made me want to puke and take a shit at the same time. I used to feel this way before exams. To be given a clue about my past was a moment I'd both dreaded and wanted. But this was more than I'd bargained for. It was one thing for Mini to tell me I was adopted and another to reveal she'd known my real father with some degree of intimacy. That she had known him, spent surreptitious hours with him in cafés swapping life stories, brought him closer in a way. She had some idea of what he was like. Had I inherited his aspects—the way he spoke, his gestures? Only she could say. I wasn't sure I was ready to have my questions answered. But I didn't have a choice. Now that Mini had built momentum, she wasn't about to stop.

When guilt got the better of her, Mini stopped seeing Burjor. She told him to run his cab elsewhere.

"I was unprepared for the strength with which the loss of his company affected me," she said.

From that moment began a long funk. Mini lost her appetite, lost weight, began to frequently take sick leave from college putting her job at risk. Getting out of bed in the morning was a task. Mini, who could read for hours at a stretch, who was a member of three libraries, found herself incapable of finishing a book. She couldn't concentrate, words wouldn't register. She grew weary of speaking, ate little, left the running of the house entirely to Ratna and retreated into a listless silence.

"Do you know what it's like to feel a hole in your chest?" Mini said. Boy, did I know. The Hole was my constant companion.

At a loss to understand her condition, Shivaji suggested she see a shrink. This was a sign of how serious Mini was for Shivaji dismissed mental illness as self-pity and psychology as a bogus discipline. The ones who truly were mentally ill, according to him, were those that needed to be institutionalized. The rest were just wallowing in a bad mood. He had only mocking things to say about Mini's friend, a therapist with a degree from the US setting up a career in Bombay at the time. Doctor Psycho is what he called her. Ratna made things worse by giving Shivaji's parents daily reports on Mini. They wanted to come to Bombay immediately and take Mini to a shaman their neighbours in Calcutta knew who, they claimed, could cure any illness. They'd have to sit around a ceremonial fire all night, he would chant and occasionally beat Mini with a broom. But it would be painless as the broom was made of peacock feathers. Shivaji, showing rare concern for Mini, stalled them. Instead he took Mini to Doctor Psycho, whose real name was Mary Tellis.

It was to her that Mini confided about Burjor and the strain of being married to a man with whom she didn't get along. Tellis suggested a period of separation to figure out whether she felt better away from Shivaji. It would be tough to live alone in Bombay on a teacher's salary but the distance might be good for her state of mind. But Mini couldn't bring herself to do something this radical.

"I thought of the scandal it would cause in the family, the shame," she said.

"Shame? What's shame when your mental health is at stake? Basically, you didn't have the balls," I said with the insolence of the young.

"Oh ya? Do you know how hard it would've been to survive on a teacher's salary? You have no idea how much things cost. Tell me, what's the price of a dozen eggs? Or a bottle of Nutella, which you eat like it's nobody's business."

About a year after they had parted, Burjor showed up. He was waiting on the street outside the building in his cab at the time Mini usually left home for college.

"For a minute, I thought what if I get into his cab and we drive away and start a new life," she said. "Should I explore the possibility of a relationship with him? Wasn't trying better than never knowing? Remember I was depressed, so I wasn't thinking clearly." Terrified of what his presence meant, Mini got into the taxi.

Turned out Burjor had married the girl from his colony he'd been seeing. She'd delivered a baby girl six months ago and died some hours after childbirth of preeclampsia. The woman had no one in Bombay, no family that could raise the child.

"He took care of you with the help of some women in the colony," Mini said. "He told me you were breastfed by a new mother in the colony who had excess milk. So much milk that she had to squeeze her breasts into the sink to get rid of the surplus."

"Breastfed by a stranger!" I said, my head in my hands. "Nourished by the proteins of another!"

"Not uncommon in certain rural communities."

Remembering that Mini couldn't have children of her own, Burjor had come to ask whether she would consider adopting me. He had an emergency of his own, which compelled him to leave town soon. Taking me along was out of the question. Could Mini give him an answer soon?

"What was the emergency?" I said.

"I don't know. But he left you clues to investigate."

8

When Mini came home in the evening of the day Burjor made his outrageous proposal, she told Shivaji she was going to adopt the child of a deceased Parsi colleague.

"Naturally, he threw a fit. 'From being depressed, you've gone crazy,' he said. I tried to use guilt. I told him, 'We can't have a child because of you. You let others believe the fault is mine *and* you don't let me adopt a baby, which is what I want most in this world. You can't have your cake and eat it too!' So he said, 'If you bring that baby into this house, I will throw both of you out!'"

"Didn't he want to meet the parent putting the kid up for adoption?' I asked her. 'Who was this colleague you'd never mentioned previously? Wasn't he suspicious? If I was him, I'd have thought this whole thing stinks."

"Forget about asking me questions, he didn't speak to me for weeks and it took four years before he could bring himself to give you a hug."

"Did you ever tell him the truth?"

"Yes, but after his spiritual turn."

Shivaji's Spiritual Turn, a major milestone in his life, occurred in the mid-eighties. Feeling sorry for himself, for having a wife who wanted different things from life, for living in this heathen city and taking orders from culturally inferior people (never mind that he himself barely read), for living with a daily reminder of his traitorous body (me), Shivaji sought solace in a series of spiritual practices. He joined a satsang group that met once a week to sing bhajans. During that period, he'd play his cassette of Krishna bhajans every morning. Not the classy stuff but songs by Bollywood playback singers set to a cheesy score of cymbals and synthesizers. Then he found a guru, who advised him to drink his own urine, a panacea for all kinds of afflictions, both physical and mental. So Shivaji began imbibing morning doses of piss, which he aimed into a cup maintained specially for the purpose.

He had a brief dalliance with Shri Homi. A Parsi godman, Homi moved around with his consort in a souped-up Fiat and delivered sermons at a maidan in Kalachowki. The two claimed to be incarnations of Shiva and Parvati. His followers wore blue felt caps and stringy ties. After a point, Shivaji had trouble taking Homi's eccentricity seriously and quit. Finally, he took to attending lectures by a religious sisterhood. From them he learned that the soul carries karmic baggage from one life to another. This meant that in a previous birth, he had committed sins that had rendered, in this life, his sperm futile. He learned that you can't change others, only yourself and that he should spend his life doing good. The period of spiritual flirtations had a pronounced effect. Shivaji grew less fussy, especially when it came to food, and occasionally took Mini's side in face-offs with Ratna.

When Mini told him about Burjor, Shivaji said nothing. Instead he spent a few days in silent contemplation. It was a tactic he'd picked up from the sisterhood. To avoid pain during a confrontation, they advised quelling the impulse to react and thinking about the issue from every possible angle. It was a principle Shivaji began applying to everything, even minor decisions and queries. Should we get an electric kettle? Is it time for new curtains? Did you take a shit this morning? The answer could take long minutes, hours, even days. At the end of his meditation, Shivaji said he forgave Mini.

"'Forgive me for what?' I said to him. I mean, it wasn't like I'd cheated on him or something."

"You might have crossed a fine line," I said.

"It was *his* doing. *He* drove me to seek friendship, intimacy—things he wasn't giving me—elsewhere. I told him, 'You should be asking *me* for forgiveness, for not telling the whole world that your balls have lost their bearings.'"

And so, I entered a household trembling with various emotional currents. Shivaji, incredulous that acquiescent Mini had actually contravened his order and brought a stranger's child home, infuriated that there was nothing he could do about it short of leaving Mini or depositing me back from where I'd come (but where had this kid really come from?). Ratna, ecstatic over the drama, dancing on her toes in anticipation of phoning her masters in Calcutta to report that the child was indeed here and that they could hop into the Howrah Mail for Bombay as they had been waiting to do ever since the news of my adoption was broken to them. But also in Ratna, an incipient feeling of something when she saw my swaddled frame. Was it maternal instinct radiating from her dormant womb? Mini, awash with love for the child of a man she had been passionate about, thrilled at her own audacity and at finally having something in this relationship that she could control.

"You had two things in your favour," Mini said. "As the offspring of a Parsi couple, there was no question of caste. Secondly, you're fair. If you were dark-skinned, your dadu-thamma would've had an issue."

In the two days it took the senior Debs to arrive from Calcutta, I had won Ratna over fully. She was prepared to mutiny against her masters if they tried to banish me, aligning with Mini for the first and only time. At last, Ratna could practice her vast knowledge of natal care lying untapped, and Mini let her, out of (a brief period of) gratitude. When I was constipated, which was often as an infant, Ratna would oil a betel leaf and lightly brush my disobedient sphincter with the suppository. When I had the runs, she would feed me a buttery mash of boiled potato and rice, the most effective jammer for a mischievous colon, rolled into spheres with fingers and palm and lined up like soldiers on my plate. She massaged my little body with mustard oil to get my circulation going and for a couple of years every day planted a black dot of kohl on my temple to ward off lurking evil eyes.

The Debs tried to persuade Mini to return me. How could she thrust a stranger's child on their son, especially since she was the one with a bad uterus? At this point, Ratna, who had overheard the fights between Mini and Shivaji, privately told Shivaji's mother that the problem was not with Mini but with Shivaji's plumbing. The doctor had suggested the issue could have something to do with his weight. But Shivaji had accepted defeat immediately, refusing to exercise or diet. Her tactic had the desired effect. The Debs, feeling responsible for their son's deleterious eating habits, backed off, going as far as to gently suggest to Shivaji that the child might repair his strained marriage. Back in Calcutta, when they told the rest of the family and friends about their adopted grandchild, they made themselves out to be progressive folk.

"Everyone there thinks you were their idea," Mini said.

They stayed for three months. Initially, they viewed me with suspicion, the way you look at a bag that has been abandoned in the train, worried it might detonate. This was partly because I was obviously not a Deb. I was too good looking, with the milky skin, fleshy features and golden-brown ringlets of a cherub gambolling in the skies of an Italian fresco. But it didn't take very long for them to warm to me and pitch in with their own ideas of child-rearing. They insisted my head be shaved at the age of two months as was customary. Mini was opposed but gave in since the Debs had accepted me. In place of my Botticellian curls, there grew limp, black hair.

"I cried when your head was shaved," Mini said. "But those two were relieved to see your new hair because it made you look less foreign."

What Mini hid from everyone, even prying Ratna, was a box of objects that came along with me. Burjor had wanted Mini to pass it on to me at an appropriate age. She gave it to me when I was eighteen, the day after my naïve confession about Danish Khan. Mini insisted I open the carton in her presence.

"I'd like some privacy," I said.

"You're such a coward you'll put it away at the back of your cupboard without looking if I leave you alone," she said.

"I might not be ready."

"You're eighteen, you're ready."

Sitting with the box before me, I recalled Kierkegaard's *The Concept of Dread*, which I had leafed through in the library in college and would read fully later on. The threshold of actions containing frightening possibilities produces a feeling of dizziness. What was I about to see? Would it answer questions about my birth parents, plugging a void that existed the moment my consciousness had come into being? Would I experience a sense of closure or greater anxiety? My head swam as I reached slowly for the box.

"Stop doing natak and open the damn thing," Mini said, leaning forward and unfolding the lid of the carton in a swift motion. Neatly arranged inside was a set of objects. An old issue of *National Geographic*, a well-worn Ricoh watch, a child's sadra, a rose-shaped mother-of-pearl broach, a postcard showing the Petit Sanatorium near Kemps Corner, a clipping of a newspaper article on Burjor, one of Bombay's few Parsi taxi drivers, and two photographs—one of Burjor lifting weights and the other, a picture of him and my mother taken in a studio. At the back of the photo was the caption, *Burjor and Armaity Elavia, 1974*. There was also a letter, written in black ink in an elegant, sloping hand in which Burjor said he had to flee Bombay after doing a terrible thing. In the letter were the names and addresses of four people who could tell me about him.

9

I was Mahtab and Moonie before I became Maya! If I felt I was being led to the precipice before being handed the box, after seeing the contents, I felt I was dangling by one foot off a ledge, gazing into a dense, swirling fog. Burjor had explained a little and offered the possibility of more answers, of meaning. Perhaps the discoveries would free me from my habitual state of fearful inertia and make me do great things in life. For what was human endeavour but a search for meaning? Kierkegaard, whose voice rang in my ears when I was confronted by existential matters, would have urged me to step off the promontory of doubt and plunge immediately into an investigation of Burjor's past by visiting those addresses.

Naturally, I did nothing. Mini and I had a good cry after reading the letter and, a few days later, I returned to Delhi, my mind in turmoil. I did nothing even though the urgency to act on my new knowledge was fanned in college by several coincidences that occurred over the following year. Friends dragged me to a production of *Oedipus*, which I watched with a lump in my throat. There was a discussion in class over the maths professor adopting a child at the late age of forty-five. When would she break it to the kid? What if the child turned out to be a dunce? I came across a tearjerker of an article in the newspaper about an Indian kid adopted by an Austrian couple, who found his birth parents in his native village at the end of a long quest. Even *Raiders of the Lost Ark*, which was screened in college one weekend, reminded me of Burjor because it's about archaeologists disinterring the past. Still, I took no action, an "incorrigible bhitu", in Mini's words, a coward. At times like this, the voice of handsome Gaurav Tripathi, the committed rationalist, rang in my ears, warning of the danger of seeking patterns in life. "By all means be spurred by these events. But resist the temptation to see these events as messages telling you to get off your ass and do something. No one's sending you messages. Not god, not Burjor's spirit. Wait, is he alive?"

At the end of 1995, we learnt Burjor had indeed been around till recently. It was the year Bombay became Mumbai. The state government, ruled by a party of cultural supremacists, decided to change the city's name as a way of showing native pride. The change was viewed as a transformation from Bombay, the liberal, welcoming immigrant city, to Mumbai, a place suspicious of outsiders, where to belong you have to know the state language. It was also the time *The Alchemist* was a rage on campus, snaring readers with trap-like pages of self-help. One of them was my flatmate Priti Singh, the bedroom evangelist.

"Believe in the universe, Maya, it will deliver," she'd say, referring to a famous line from the book.

"Deliver what?"

"What you most desire."

"What I desire right now is to be delivered from this nightmare to find that Bombay is still Bombay."

"Just believe."

What the universe did offer up was a phone call from Nepal. Mini called at night to give me the news. The owner of a lodge in Kathmandu had phoned to tell Mini that Burjor had died. He'd been staying there for about a decade, making a living running some kind of import-export business. He'd seemed fine that day, stepping out for breakfast, making calls, sitting by the window in the lobby for an afternoon nap. On days there was a nip in the air, he liked to doze with the sun on his face. When he'd been stationery for more than an hour—he usually didn't nap for more than twenty minutes—the owner of the lodge shook his shoulder. Burjor, his legs crossed, his arms folded, his face angled towards the sun had passed "just like a gentleman" the owner told Mini. He had found Mini's number in Burjor's phonebook in a brief list of important numbers.

How do you grieve for a parent you never knew? Was it grief over his death I felt or dismay that I had done nothing about investigating Burjor while he was alive? I could've tracked him down, established a relationship, heard stories of his adventurous life. Perhaps knowing him would have filled the emptiness in me, inciting me to do great things. But—this was a good thing—I had to set my mixed-up feelings aside and console Mini, who was beside herself. Sitting in my room in Bombay and trying to be quiet so that neither Shivaji nor Ratna would hear her, Mini gave me the news in between sobs. The force of her reaction startled me; I thought the analgesic distance of years had dimmed her passion for him. But when I reflected on it later on, it seemed to me that Mini was mourning Burjor and, by extension, her former life. Her brief dalliance with Burjor and the fantasy of a life more exciting and loving than the one she had with Shivaji. Bombay's new identity would have had deeper meaning for Mini for it meant the end of a certain character of the city, a change that was set in motion by the riots in 1992, and the conclusive end to the headiest period of her life.

Over the next few weeks, Mini called me often, wanting to talk about Burjor. She remembered things about him that she hadn't thought of in years. His body, which she could tell by the snug fit of his clothes, was fit. When she shyly asked him whether he worked out, he told her he'd lifted weights for years, first at a physical culture centre, a gym as it was known in the fifties and sixties, and later at home. She remembered his intelligence, his sharp observations of people, his street savviness. He knew the prices of everything, knew all about getting licences and permissions for all sorts of things. He knew the four major languages spoken in

Bombay—Hindi, Marathi, Gujarati and English—and seamlessly switched accents and idioms depending on who he was talking to. With Mini, his English was polished for a cabbie, though the odd mispronunciation or grammatical error gave away his lack of education, and with the Goan waiter of a restaurant, Burjor would slip into Bombay's peculiar street English. When Burjor paid attention, he had a direct, unmoving gaze, which was unnerving because one is used to nodding listeners, but also sweet as he seemed to be absorbing every little detail of what she was saying, as opposed to Shivaji, who was usually uninterested in anything she had to say. A vague outline of Burjor began to form. It would be coloured later on with details that would surprise and delight me and shock Mini, who actually knew very little.

I resolved to look up the people Burjor had listed in his letter when I was home for the holidays. But when I went home, there was always stuff to do. Friends to meet, books to read for the next term, time to be wasted with Kersi over pot. The impulse to find Burjor waned and the years passed. Meanwhile, the feeling of being adrift grew stronger. I took up an internship at the paper, a job that began leaching my intelligence from the start. But continued as a full-fledged employee, for work added ballast to life and gave me an excuse to take no fear-inducing decisions.

It took thirteen years to get me started. Two events occurred in 2008, one of which was the siege on 26th November.

10

A month before the attack, I happened to be scanning various newspapers at work. It was early afternoon, the newsroom was quiet, the silence interrupted by Purnendu banging away at his computer as he muttered under his breath. "Bhenchod, useless fellow." I was leafing through a paper that few, aside from veteran Parsis, read. Every day half a page was devoted to Parsiana, advertisements issued by community groups, articles on Parsis and their issues. An obituary of one Keki Mehta caught my eye. A successful manufacturer of masalas, Mehta grew up in poverty in a village in Gujarat. His wife, who was interviewed for the piece, was quoted saying that Mehta did various odd jobs in Bombay before securing a loan from a small-time businessman, who looked out for poor Parsis, called Burjor Elavia. That set Mehta off. He began making masalas from recipes he'd learned in Gujarat and selling them.

"Maya, machher chop khabi? Barir banano," Purnendu called out from his desk. Do you want a fish chop? It's homemade.

"Na."

"Na? Theek achhish to? Number two korishni aajke?" Are you alright? Didn't take a dump today?

At that moment, my gut was clenched so tight not the minutest turd could've passed through its coils. Seeing Burjor's name was as shocking as seeing a person who you'd thought was long dead taking a stroll in front of you. I was Hamlet staring at my father's ghost. How many people out there knew Burjor? How many were alive? When did Burjor, a documented cab driver, become a businessman with enough capital to dole out loans? Over years of inaction, Burjor had assumed an imaginary quality. He was a secret held by me and Mini. So, it was almost unthinkable that there were others out there who knew of him. Once the blunt force of spotting Burjor's name abated somewhat, I felt fired up by the mystery. If I failed to act immediately, as I had repeatedly done in the past, I would forever suffer this pallid life.

The following day, I began to look for Homi Sukhadia. As there was no number, I turned up at the address, a chawl in Byculla, not far from the zoo. From the looks of it, the people living there had done well. There were signs of upwardly mobile middle-class life in the homes, which were arranged around common balconies and open to scrutiny; few front doors were closed. A Muslim family lived in the two-room house Sukhadia had occupied. They'd never heard of him and suggested I call the landlord, whose family had owned the building for generations. The man, Altaf Arsiwala, lived just down the road in a building and I went over that very day. Arsiwala, eighty years old and arthritic, lived with his male help and rarely had visitors. When I showed up looking for Sukhadia, Arsiwala was delighted. At last, here was an adventure, something to look forward to. His wife had died some years ago, his kids were settled abroad and came down once a year if he was lucky and his relatives in Bombay looked in on him once in a while out of reluctant duty, for who wanted to spend free time, precious in this city, with an old, bow-legged man whose inflamed joints made movement painfully slow.

"Basically, everyone is waiting for me to die," he said, as his factotum brought me tea and khari biscuits.

I figured it would be a while before Arsiwala would tell me what I'd come to find out. Starved of human company, he was in the mood to talk, less about my mission than about himself. Arsiwala's family had been in the business of arsis, mirrors. The walls of his living room were hung with several of them, each with an elaborate frame, and pictures of his wife.

"The idea is that from wherever I stand, I should be able to see a reflection of Sakina," he said. "When you grow old, you develop all kinds of eccentricities. Others get annoyed so I suppose it's best that no one comes. I like sitting on this chair only. If a guest sits, I make the person get up. They think I'm strange."

The other business had been glass objects. In

the living room were a couple of cabinets filled with containers of all shapes and sizes, cut work vials for perfume, milk jugs, ice-cream cups, bowls, teacups, sauce boats, inkwells, paperweights, decanters, vases, water bottles. Usually, mirrors and glass give small rooms the illusion of space. In this case, the profusion of the stuff made the room look smaller, the reflected walls appearing to close in on themselves. Before me was Arsiwala and my distracting image in a mirror. Perhaps, I thought, Arsiwala liked living in this oppressive hall of mirrors because it gave the illusion that there were more people in the house.

"You see, I'm a lover of poetry," he said, in a mix of English and Hindi. "I see glass, not just as a means of livelihood, but as a metaphor of the human being. Both have strength and fragility."

The businesses had been started by his father, a migrant from Surat. Arsiwala sold it when the arthritis got unbearable.

"Plus my kids didn't want to be 'shopkeepers'," he said. "They think business is dirty. One of them has started a tech company in San Francisco. He sells advice on how to take care of pets and calls himself an entrepreneur. You pay to find out how to deworm your dog or deal with a moody cat, stuff you find for free on Google. I told him, 'Boss, you can call yourself any fancy thing but you're still doing dhanda, business only. And I don't know what kind of nonsense business this is. You'll fail and then come to me for money, money that has been made selling these beautiful objects, not some useless, intangible thing'."

The glass business had done well and senior Arsiwala had bought a couple of buildings, the chawl in Byculla and an old apartment block in Bohri mohalla.

"They're like stones around my neck," he said. Like most landlords of old buildings in the city, Arsiwala couldn't afford to maintain his properties. He made peanuts in rent since prices were frozen by Rent Control. The building in Bohri mohalla, a century-old wooden structure, could collapse any day, he said. The Byculla chawl was better off since the tenants paid for the upkeep.

"It wasn't like it is now in Sukhadia's time," Arsiwala said, finally coming down to it. "Back then, I won't hesitate to say, it was a pathetic place."

Sukhadia had got community housing somewhere in Fort. That's all Arsiwala knew. Before I left, he took my number and said he would call me once in a while, if that was alright, to check whether I'd found my man. I'd told him that Sukhadia was a long-lost family friend.

"He was a quiet fellow," Arsiwala said. "I don't know what he did but I had the feeling it wasn't a regular job. We didn't ask too many questions as long as we got our rent."

From the palpable loneliness of Arsiwala's hall of mirrors, I dived straight into the afternoon chaos of work. As usual, Purnendu was hoovering a plate of food and huddling with his Bengali lackeys. It was the BMC reporter's birthday and every year as a treat, she ordered kebabs and pao for the newsroom from Firdos in Crawford Market.

The only person I knew with connections to the community housing board was the health reporter, Mahrukh Marolia. She was a veteran of the place and feted for her reportage, especially a long-running series on public hospitals. Now she'd been a good reporter back in the day, for kids starting out in the field she was still a good mentor. But now she had it easy. Every day a Right to Information activist would come to her with a scandal. She'd get a few quotes, make a half-assed attempt at corroborating the story and voila, front-page lead. To be sure, she was likeable. She cracked funny jokes and was generous with her kheema cutlets. The only thing she didn't have a sense of humour about was religion. The woman had serious faith. She and Adi Sanjana, the front-page editor, would occasionally spar over the issue of the Zoroastrian orthodoxy being hung up on keeping the bloodline pure. Mahrukh couldn't get over the fact that Sanjana, who came from a priestly family and who had himself trained as a junior priest, whose name signalled that he was from Sanjan, one of the first Indian ports on which fleeing Zoroastrians had set foot, had married a Punjabi.

"There's no such thing as pure blood, Mahrukh. You think those Sassanians only bonked each other or what? Soon there won't be enough Parsis left. What will you do then? Tell the kids to marry their brothers and sisters and have messed up babies like the Egyptians? Why do you think Tutankhamun was lame?"

"There's the IVF programme and the community gives money to couples who have more than one child. These initiatives could work you know," Mahrukh said.

"Some two babies a year come out of that programme. And twenty people die in a year. Please find the brain that you once used to apply to your job and do the math."

"You have to have faith Adi."

"You know who else gives a fuck about pure blood? Fascists. The goddamn neo-Nazis. You two have something in common."

Now Mahrukh wasn't crazy about me. She thought I tended to assert my voice at the expense of hers when I edited her stories. The times I'd asked for her supporting quotes or more information, she'd yelled at me in full view of the newsroom. "Don't act too smart, young lady," she'd shouted, her boxy, square-shouldered body and halo of wiry hair vibrating, like a rocket about to take off. On a couple of occasions, she'd complained to Adi and Daniel Chacko, the resident editor. Chacko, a highly intelligent but entirely gutless individual, pandered to Mahrukh. His great fear was that his best journalists would defect to other papers even though it was obvious they weren't going anywhere. This was too cushy a job. Chacko told me to be mindful of

Mahrukh's experience and careful while editing. Adi was straightforward. "Mahrukh, you're a front-page story mill and we love you for that. But let's face it, you're not a writer. You have basic problems with grammar. No one's blaming you because it's not your fault; your parents sent you to a third-rate school. So just let Maya do her job okay."

I had no choice but to ask Mahrukh to help me with Sukhadia. As a trade-off, I'd have to be lenient with a few of her pieces, let some of the puns she was so fond of pass. "The government hospital is literally in a soup as fifty patients fell ill after having the vegetable soup served for lunch on Monday." She was suspicious, not fully buying my story—my folks were trying to trace an old friend who they'd heard had fallen on hard times. Could Mahrukh work her contacts to get me an address or number?

"Has Adi put you up to this? I know he's been trying to get someone to do a piece on poor Parsis on the housing wait list," she said.

"What? No, of course not."

"That would be very sneaky. I mean I can understand Adi's concern but he's biased. On the face of it, these people have been waiting for years to get houses while those who are wealthier pay and get flats in south Bombay colonies. But it's more complicated and I don't want any bad press."

"Listen Mahrukh, this is a personal thing. I'm not chasing a story. I swear on my unborn children."

She sniggered. “You’re in your mid-thirties. No husband. No boyfriend also na? At this rate, you’re not having any children.”

A few days later, Mahrukh handed me a slip of paper with a landline number and an address.

11

When the number went unanswered a couple of times, I went over one morning before work. The address was for a building in one of the lanes off Shahid Bhagat Singh Road near the General Post Office. Old buildings with shops and businesses like logistics and metal works line the shabby street. I entered one such block, whose floors were propped up from the inside with bamboo poles. A wooden staircase that felt delicate wound upstairs and as I climbed gingerly I saw various enterprises operating out of flats and passages—a tailoring workshop, a printer of wedding cards, a courier service. The stairwell was dark, sunlight filtered in through small, grime-smeared windows and I had the feeling I was ascending levels of a subterranean sphere. On the topmost floor was a flat bearing Sukhadia's name on the door. The bell went unanswered.

I went back the following day. The wedding card printer told me Sukhadia was out. He was out the next afternoon as well. I rang a few times but there was no answer. Sukhadia was mighty busy for an old guy.

On the night of 26th November, I went over to Sukhadia's. I'd wrapped up early that evening and by the time I got to his building, a five-minute cab ride from work, it was quarter to nine. As soon as I entered, the printer, who was packing a large consignment of wedding cards near the stairs, announced that Sukhadia had just stepped out. He'd gone to the station to meet someone at Refresh, a cafeteria. If I walked quickly, I might overtake him. But I had no idea what he looked like. The printer told me Sukhadia was in a red t-shirt and that he had light grey eyes.

Obviously, it was a fool's mission. The roads were full of people streaming to the station, Sukhadia could've been on either side of the road leading to the General Post Office and from there left to the station. Nevertheless, I walked to CST, scanning the streets for men in red t-shirts. I took the closest entrance, the one near the long distance train platforms, thinking Sukhadia would do the same thing. It was around nine twenty at night. I entered the station and walked a few steps in the direction of Refresh when the staccato of what could either be gunshots or crackers rang out. Then I heard screams, saw some commotion in the distance and I turned and fled the station, running down the path to the gate and from there right towards the office. By the time I reached, word had arrived that gunmen had stormed the station. Soon afterwards, we heard of the attacks on Cama Hospital, the Taj, Oberoi.

I was reeling from what I'd seen, fielding phone calls

from editors and out of my mind with worry for Homi when Mini called. Wailing, she told me that Shivaji was trapped in the Taj. He'd gone for the wedding of his boss's son. She was watching the vaudevillian coverage on television and weeping. I could hear Ratna's hysterics in the background.

How was one to digest this outrageous set of events? Burjor's name delivered in the papers. (Immediately Gaurav Tripathi's voice rang out: It was a coincidence Maya; his name wasn't "delivered" by the great postman in the sky. This is how delusions begin, in language. Tripathi, this is not the right time.) Beginning my investigation at last. Homi snatched away when I'd almost found him. Shivaji at risk of being shot to death by terrorists. The only father I'd known at the risk of being felled not by cancer or the chance impact of a tree branch weakened by the monsoon but in the most theatrical blitz in the city's history...

Shivaji was rescued twelve hours later in an operation orchestrated by the hotel's head chef. I must have hugged him voluntarily for the first time, communicating through the long embrace the intense relief of seeing him alive. Then, leaving him to the eager ministrations of Ratna and Mini, I plunged back into the chaotic whorl of the attack to find Homi. An unfamiliar fever took hold of me. Finding Homi assumed a life-saving urgency. I was saving myself and there was nothing I'd pursued so far with such excitement.

Had he made it to the station at all? Perhaps he had

escaped the bullets or turned around when he heard the screams or perhaps he'd stopped at a shop or a café along the way and hadn't made it to the station till after the terrorists had fled. He could be sitting at home watching the attack unfold on the telly. I went to his building. The doorbell went unanswered and I was told that he hadn't been seen since the previous day. I pestered the reporters for details of survivors, their names, which hospitals the injured had been taken to. When the attack came to an end, I accompanied reporters to government hospitals to interview the injured. It was in the general ward of St George's Hospital, in the racket of patients, their relatives, squalling children, that I found Homi. He was lying still, corpse-like, his bed a hushed island in an ocean of noise. He wasn't as badly off as the others, I was told. A bullet had grazed him and he'd had a solid concussion. When I touched his arm, he opened his eyes. Light grey eyes, just as the wedding card printer had said, in a toffee-coloured face.

He looked at me steadily for a few moments, then said, "Moonie."

12

Homi, who I soon began calling Homi uncle, was ready to talk a week after being discharged. This time he answered the doorbell, led me into a small, tidily kept flat and proceeded to talk to me, in a mix of so-so English and Gujarati, as if we'd known each other for years. What had taken me so long? I was expected ages ago, as soon as I'd become an adult. Lucky for me, he was still around. The bullet could've got him and this building could get him any day. It was in danger of caving in and every time he took the stairs, he thought the vibrations would trigger a collapse. He'd applied for community housing but those guys were yet to move on his plea. Did I want some tea? He'd make me tea the Parsi way, with mint, lemongrass and ginger.

As he disappeared into the kitchen, I tried to wrap my head around the strange feeling of having a history with Homi Sukhadia but without being able to recall any of it. How could I? I was just a few months old when Burjor gave me to Mini. Yet, here was Homi behaving as though I was a niece visiting from a foreign country after years, calling me by a childhood name I'd learned about only as an adult.

The room had a divan that I guess doubled up as a bed, a cushioned, two-seat sofa, on which I sat, a couple of chairs, a trunk for a coffee table, a television and a steel cupboard. What did his lack of possessions say about him? That he was unsentimental or that he was used to moving around? There were no knick-knacks, no picture frames, nothing useless. Sukhadia brought a tray with two cups of chai and a plate of two kinds of biscuits, khari and nankhatai.

"OK, so where to start? Let's see," he said, rubbing his hands.

There was no preliminary chatter, no questions about my life or why I'd only just decided to get in touch, just a disconcerting familiarity. He started immediately, from the very beginning.

Burjor was born in 1935 in a village near Vansda in Gujarat to a Parsi businessman and tribal woman. It was common at the time for Parsi landowners with businesses out in the sticks to have tribal mistresses.

"They were bastards, I tell you. Myself, I had a Parsi father and tribal mother. My eyes and nose, as you can see, are his. She died young and he sent me to a boarding school. Never saw him after age ten."

Mr Elavia—Homi didn't remember Burjor's father's name—ran the family liquor business and divided his time between Navsari, where he lived with his wife and kids, and the outskirts of Vansda, where he had distilleries. He sold country liquor, brewed from mahua flowers, and toddy and owned a few shops. He was also a big landowner, having amassed vast tracts of farmland over the years, largely from debt-ridden peasants. According to Homi, Parsi liquor barons historically had a reputation for being rapacious, selling booze on credit to farmers and seizing their lands when they couldn't afford to pay back. Elavia, Homi said, was particularly venal. He'd get tribal farmers to labour on their farms, the ones he'd snatched, and pay them with liquor. Surprisingly, he was good to Burjor. When Burjor was ten, Elavia took him home to Navsari, to live with his family and put him in a decent school.

"The problem was Elavia's wife. She hated Burjor. I mean, naturally. This was common back then but no woman likes it when her husband cheats na? On top of that, he brought home the evidence."

"What about Burjor's mother?"

"He saw her on and off. She drank herself to an early death."

When Elavia was away in Vansda, his wife treated Burjor like dirt. After school, he was made to wash dishes, dust the furniture, run errands and so on. He had two grown-up half-siblings, a brother, who despised him thinking he would claim their father's legacy, and a sister, who was kind. She tutored him and thwarted her mother when the woman got into a rage and raised a hand on Burjor.

"You know why? She was a good soul and all, and

she was in love with a man like us. He was a teacher in Burjor's school. Lived and looked like a Parsi. Not many knew that his navjote had not been done, so technically he was an outsider. Burjor was their courier. He would deliver his sister's letters to the masterji and the masterji's letters to his sister. Whether they got married or what, who knows."

At the age of eighteen, sick of being shoved around by his stepmother and the small town oppressiveness of Navsari, Burjor left for Bombay. Elavia was loath to see him go, Sukhadia said. The old man was fond of Burjor and guilty over his wife's behaviour. In his old age, Elavia, stricken with severe arthritis, practically bedridden, his fingers bent and claw-like, was entirely dependent on his wife. Homi saw the illness as divine comeuppance for all the lives Elavia had crushed. It was Burjor's job to bathe him, clean him when he took a shit, and when he pissed his pants, which was often for the old man was incontinent. A grateful Elavia protested when his wife treated Burjor badly but he was too feeble to do more than admonish her. So Burjor took the money Elavia pressed on him—"0.0001 per cent of his inheritance," according to Homi—and left for Bombay.

Now unlike his sister's paramour, Burjor was an initiate. In 1942, when he was seven, Burjor had been a part of a historic, mass navjote organized by S, a man from the village, "a fifty-fifty like Burjor and me", who had for years unsuccessfully lobbied with various influential Parsis to get the community to acknowledge the fifty-fifties. A famous priest from Bombay and ten junior priests initiated seventy-seven boys, girls and adults over three days on the porch of a village home near Vansda. Burjorji Bharucha, a social worker from Bombay, a disciple of Gandhi and friend of Nehru, had helped see the whole thing through. S was himself part of the ceremony. After years of wearing a sadra without a kusti, the custom among fifty-fifties, he was able to tie the thread around his waist. A whole lot of conservative folk were opposed to the navjote. On the day the priests arrived from Bombay, two stick-wielding Parsis went to receive them at the station.

"They wanted to scare them away. But the fools, when they saw ten strong, healthy priests get down from the train, they only got scared and ran away!"

"What about you?" I asked.

After the navjote of 1942, it became more common for fifty-fifties—the word lodged itself in my head—to be taken into the Zoroastrian fold. Homi, who was younger than Burjor, had been in a smaller group navjote.

"If you go to some villages even now, you'll find poor families who have dark skin and adivasi features. But they have names like Dinshaw and Eruch."

It was time to go to work. If I'd known what I was in for, I'd have taken the day off. Homi protested; he wasn't even halfway through.

"Burjor's life was like a Hindi picture. This is not even the interval."

When we said goodbye, I had the same feeling I'd experienced at Arsiwala's door, that I was collecting a father figure. Homi saw me off with the same mixture of neediness and paternal affection. There was also hesitation, which I read as him trying not to burden me with his expectations. Did he hope I'd continue our association after he'd told me everything, assume the role of a niece or goddaughter? We fixed up to meet earlier the next day. We'd start at breakfast, continue over lunch and if I had to, I'd call Purnendu to tell him I had "pet kharab", an upset stomach, and I couldn't stray too far from the toilet.

13

From being a rootless individual, I was now being told I belonged to a history that involved savage liquor barons, adivasi women, a scandalous navjote. This was off the wall! What a story to regale people with at a party—my grandfather, an unscrupulous landlord and philanderer; my father, the unfortunate offspring of his father's transgressions, raised by a tyrannical stepmother, flees to Bombay like so many millions of impoverished people, drives a cab... Yet, the knowledge did nothing to dispel the discombobulating feeling of having emerged from a void, of learning about a past of which I had no memory. Would it have made a difference had I heard these stories at Burjor's knee instead of second-hand as an adult?

Not long back, Tumpa and I had a conversation about making art from the mundane. We often had an early lunch before work at a place close to the office. That day we were at Café Excelsior, making our way through bheja fry, goat brain veiled by a thick omelette, kheema pao and Irani chai.

"If you're black or dalit or your roots lie in some remote tribal hamlet in the Himalayas, you belong to a tradition that you can finagle for stories," I complained. "It doesn't matter if you've never known racism or been stopped from drinking at a brahmin's well. There's a readymade narrative right there. Don't they say that you should start by writing about yourself? Well, I don't have a fucking start."

"Who says?" said Tumpa, quickly masticating the chewy pao and mince into a paste that filled the crevices of her teeth and flew occasionally across the table to fleck my face. The food was so good it was impossible to be leisurely.

"People, the pundits of writing."

"What about developing an interest in something other than yourself?"

"I could. But I'd be more invested in a story connected to me in some way. Perhaps, like Schiller, I need a drawer full of rotten apples whose sweet stench of decay will compel me to write."

"See boss, I don't know about Schiller-viller. But I agree, you need some heavy-duty julab for the brain. I'll tell you what your problem is. You're fucking lazy. This lack of a personal story has become an excuse to do nothing and to feel sorry about yourself. Kindly use your considerable brain to lift yourself out of the rut you're in or your bheja will get fried like this thing here."

Now I'd begun to discover that I did indeed have

an exciting past, a revelation that delivered both joy and dread. Would it be the spur that I craved?

These thoughts skated through my mind as I wrapped up work and made my way to the annual office party. The timing was convenient. Typically, everyone in the newsroom let loose to an embarrassing degree. A whole lot of food and drink was consumed, there was dancing and all that churning caused alimentary upheavals. Purnendu Purukayastha, the city editor, would believe me if I said I was too sick to come to work the following day, leaving me the whole day with Homi.

Since it was 2009, the year after the financial crisis, funds were tight. Instead of the usual posh place, a smaller bar was booked for the party. The theme of the place was American Prohibition. There were murals of men in fedoras and boxy suits on the walls and the menu had cocktails like Bee's Knees and Mary Pickford. Purnendu was warmed up by the time I got there, after putting the next day's edition to bed. Tumpa told me that the DJ had optimistically started with jazz but after being booed, had switched to Bollywood without the usual Michael Jackson-Madonna interlude.

"Why American Prohibition?" Purnendu wanted to know. "Why not Bombay Prohibition? We had it for so many years. If I were to start a bar, I'd serve desi daru cocktails. Bloody Mariam. Satara Sling. Madras Mule."

"One leaf of lettuce sends you running to the loo," Tumpa said. "Forget about desi daru boss."

"Tui last dui nombor kobe korli?" When did you last shit? "Three days ago? One week? That's why you're full of gas today. I had to rewrite your story. Ask Maya."

Purnendu and his crew of sycophants were openly ogling the new civic reporter, a leggy Punjabi called Lovely Singh, who having grown up in Nagpur, spoke faultless Marathi, startling everyone in her first week at work. She was being swung on the dance floor by the business editor, Raj Ranganathan, who we called Randy Raju, which became R2, which became R2D2 owing to a Star Wars fan in the newsroom. In the hope of meeting single women, R2D2 had joined a weekend salsa class some years ago, becoming proficient enough to participate in minor competitions. Though he was yet to meet single women through this route. Every office party, R2D2 would pull a new reporter, too shy to say no, on to the dance floor no matter what kind of music was playing. In the scene that ensued, R2D2 would expertly move while flicking his clumsy, flailing partner around. Lovely Singh, Butter Chicken to Purnendu and his cronies, tried to be good humoured as R2D2 rolled her into his chest and flung her out.

"Boombada, Butter Chicken ke dekechho? Phataphati lagchhe aajke," one of them said. Have you seen Butter Chicken? She looks hot today.

"Uff, khete ichhe korchhe," Purnedu said. I want to eat her.

"Butter Chicken-e khoob moshla kintu. Tomar shojjo hobena. Khele shesh," Tumpa said. There's too much masala in butter chicken. Eat it and you're dead.

"Someone bring air freshener. This Tumpa is farting too much today."

I parked myself near Thomas D'Mello, an old timer who wrote op-eds. He wore a bow tie, suspenders and canvas shoes and looked like he'd just been at the races. Truly, no one left this paper; it was a living museum in which you could see the evolution of the Indian journalist. Thomas was blind, and very wise. Or perhaps his blindness made him seem enlightened. Whatever the case, he was sought out for his counsel by people at work; some claimed he was clairvoyant and gave him the nickname Saint Thomas. Whenever I looked in his direction, I saw Thomas staring attentively with his unseeing eyes at some troubled individual. The newsroom's Tiresias. Thomas was facing the dance floor with a grin that suggested he could see what R2D2 was up to. In his hand was a glass of port wine, more accurately, the sickly sweet fortified alcohol that was passed off as port.

"Saint Thomas, how do you drink this piss?" I said.

"It reminds me of my salad days. Back then, you didn't have much choice. I remember going to aunty bars in Dhobi Talao with my friends during Prohibition and drinking cheap liquor brewed from god knows what." The coincidence of Thomas bringing up illicit booze on the day I'd learned that my grandfather had been ruthless liquor dealer made me alert.

"Tell me more."

"The places were called aunty bars because they were run by Catholic 'aunties' in their homes. Their husbands were drunks, good-for-nothings. Once my friends and I nearly got caught. Cops raided the bar we were in and we had to scram out of the backdoor. What an adventure I tell you!"

"Where was the stuff made?"

"In the outskirts, places like Andheri and Vasai. Can you imagine Andheri was the back of beyond then? They came up with all kinds of ways to transport the booze. Concealing liquor in rubber tyres was popular. If you ever do a story on Prohibition, talk to me. I can give you so many anecdotes."

"Tell me some now."

"I would, but Selvam is here."

I turned around to see Selvam, Thomas's long-time steward, who had arrived to take his boss home.

"How did you know?" I said.

"Maya, just because I'm blind doesn't mean my other senses don't function," Thomas said enigmatically as he left.

It was past one thirty in the morning but the cops did the paper a favour by letting the party continue. The bacchanal had begun its descent into chaos. A few people had thrown up in the loo; one of Boomba's smarmy minions cast aside all inhibition to ask an openly lesbian editor how, as a woman, she could feel satisfied with pussy; Boomba was doing the chicken dance in his corner; Lovely Singh had been commandeered by a drunk Daniel Chacko, the skirt-chasing resident editor; R2D2 was a top spinning out of control.

14

The morning after the office party, I met Homi uncle down the road from his home, at Café Universal. "Moonie!" he called out and gave me a hug, for which I was unprepared, being hungover and as yet unused to my new situation. The fondness in Homi's eyes killed me. He ordered bun maska and chai, I got an omelette and a side of cheese balls, needing the steadying effect of grease.

"Didn't sleep or what?" he said.

"Not much. There was an office party."

"Oh ho!" he said, mimicking the action of drinking from a bottle.

As we ate, Homi picked up from where he'd left off the previous day. Burjor left Navsari for Bombay soon after he turned eighteen, in 1953. His sister's boyfriend, the schoolteacher, hooked him up with a friend living in Petit Sanatorium near Kemps Corner. But since the sanatorium, the same one pictured on the postcard in the box, was meant to temporarily shelter Parsis, Burjor didn't have long to live there. His first job was cleaning and serving at an Irani café in Dhobi Talao. The café opened around five in the morning for people on their way to bet at the races. This meant Burjor had to be up at dawn to help with the baking of pao and work all day till the evening. At night he slept in the shop. The job went on for months—till he was caught making out with the café owner's daughter.

"Frankly speaking, I don't know how he found the time," Homi said. "But then we're talking about Burjor. He was a ladies' man. What I'm telling you about the Irani's daughter is what he told me. But I have seen with my own eyes how girls used to look at him and how he used to patao them. Don't get me wrong—Burjor was a decent guy. He loved women, of all kinds. He wasn't some dirty roadside Romeo type. But yes, he got into trouble because of women. Biggest trouble was with your real mummy. Got her pregnant and then had to marry her."

"How'd he get caught?"

"He and this Irani's daughter, who by the way was ten years older than him, were doing chumma-chaati in one lane near the café. Someone who knew her father saw them and went straight to the Irani. The Irani gave Burjor two slaps and threw him out."

Burjor, who had no intention of being a waiter for long, had already been working on his next career move. One of the regulars at the café owned a bunch of taxis and was frequently in need of drivers. In the evenings, Burjor took lessons from one of the guy's drivers. By the time he was kicked out, Burjor was ready to drive a cab.

After breakfast, we decided to walk around Ballard Estate. It was my suggestion for my head was a delicate globe throbbing from the long-lasting effects of cheap alcohol and the information Homi issued in the stoic style of a 1980s newsreader. He was narrating Burjor's story with single-minded focus as though divesting himself of a precious object in his safe-keeping on to the intended recipient. However, the intended recipient wasn't ready to receive it all at once. The intended recipient was having a hard time swallowing the cheese balls, normally addictive, and was sitting with her head in the palm of one hand, as if propping her brain drooping from the weight of this story. Yet Homi, the rug-puller, noticed none of this and ploughed on.

Meanwhile, I tried to absorb the idea that soon after arriving in Bombay, eighteen-year-old Burjor had begun a career as a Casanova by seducing an older woman. An older woman! This suggested a degree of sexual maturity. Had he had any experience in Navsari? In between homework, doing the dishes and nursing his bedridden father, would Burjor skip out to the town's lover's lane to squeeze some girl's tits? So far, I knew of the Irani, my biological mother—who he knocked up, making me a goddamn mistake!—and Mini. How many others had this rustic Lothario charmed?

We walked down Adi Marzban Path towards Ballard Estate. Adi Marzban, the Parsi-Gujarati playwright considered a genius for his double entendre-filled comedies, had a part to play in Burjor's story, about which I'd learn later on. The queasiness I felt ebbed inside the Edwardian grid of Ballard Estate. As always, the solid stone buildings had a sedative effect on my nerves. And, as if a predetermined programme clicked into motion, I began my tour guide routine.

"See Homi uncle, I don't know if you know but the area in which you live came up in the early 1900s when land was reclaimed for the Alexandra Docks. The reason some of these streets are named Cochin and Calicut was because of the maritime trade between the cities. Let's turn left and walk towards Grand Hotel."

Homi looked at me with admiration and affection, making me wish I'd kept my mouth shut. "So much you know, Moonie. You know Burjor used to tell me he fell in love with Bombay as a taxi driver. He loved to drive around and see things. You have the same love for the city. It must be his influence."

"How would he have influenced me?"

"His spirit, Moonie. Burjor's spirit is sending you vibrations. My guru says people don't die, they transform into different energies."

"Who's your guru?"

"He's called Homi, like me. Shri Homi."

Shri Homi, the same crackpot Shivaji had taken to during his spiritual phase in the eighties. If I brought it up, Homi would no doubt interpret the coincidence as a divine convergence.

"Yeah, I read about the guy. I read he was investigated for tax fraud."

"Tax fraud on the surface. Actually, it was a conspiracy against him by evil energies. But it's over and done with. Guruji's aura is too powerful, no one can touch him."

"So Burjor started driving a cab. Then what?"

The first cab was a Hillman Minx, which belonged to a seth who owned several taxis. For some time, Burjor lived in the man's garage and did odd jobs aside from driving the cab. There he met a fellow driver, Madhu Pereira, who had a lucrative side gig brewing liquor. Pereira, an East Indian, came from a village in Vasai, where it was common for families to make arrack from fruit. So he had the tools and the know-how. What he needed was a partner. Prohibition was in place at the time and there was much demand for cheap booze. Burjor, who was always looking for ways to make quick money, jumped at the chance. The job wasn't entirely new for Burjor. He'd been to his father's distillery in Vansda, he knew the basics of working a crude still. Madhu Pereira and Burjor would drive their taxis to swamps in Vasai, Andheri, Juhu, where brewers made liquor from rotting vegetables and fruit. They'd hide the hellish stuff in tyres and transport it to clandestine bars around the city. Some of them were the 'aunty' bars Thomas had told me about.

"It was a natural fit. Booze was his family dhanda plus Burjor enjoyed anything slightly shady. He was an ek number ka admi who liked doing do number ka kaam."

We walked past Grand Hotel, past Britannia, where I stepped in to take away a caramel custard. A cat was curled at the till, where once the owner's soda-drinking pet rooster, immortalized on the paper napkins, had stood. We halted at the circle with the lamp post marking the Bombay Port Trust's involvement in World War 1 and fixed a date to meet a couple of weeks later. This time, Homi was in a hurry to leave. He was off to catch a train to "see his people" in Gujarat and said he would explain later.

15

After parting from Homi, I made my way to Colaba to meet Tumpa. On the way, an old memory surfaced. Homi had mentioned Burjorji Bharucha, the social worker who'd helped put together the navjote at which Burjor was initiated. I remembered Karl Kudva telling the class Bharucha's story.

Kudva was our English teacher and one of two male teachers in school. We called him Karela because the karela, bitter gourd, is kadva, bitter. Back then Karela had a handsome, craggy face framed by a head of wavy hair and a slender goatee. The word was that he was seeing Charulata Choksi, the history teacher, who with her gamine frame, pixie hair and almond eyes was a real bomb. She wore shirts tucked into drainpipes that moulded a pert bum, which we girls considered the eidos of pert bums. If they were seeing each other, it was obviously a tumultuous relationship since Choksi was often seen red-nosed, wet-eyed with the school's agony aunt, the librarian Agnes Gomes.

He was the only reason we made it through *As*

You Like It. Not because he looked good, though naturally, that helped. But because he had the knack of making even a frothy romance about cross-dressing boys and girls capering in a forest interesting. It was his voice, sandpapered to a deep, rough timbre by years of smoking, the way he walked up and down gesturing, his whole body a bellow breathing life into the text. He drew connections between the literature we studied and other books, films, plays. He threw names at us like confetti and those of us who cared would take notes and run to the library to look up Sebald, Dostoevsky, Naipaul.

Karela taught us the history of Bombay that was nowhere in our textbooks. The Samyukta Maharashtra Movement, the formation of the Shiv Sena, the history of labour in the city. He told us about his brief dalliance with the Communist Party of India as a youth activist and his longer association with a Leftist theatre group. He quit because he was more suited to being "an armchair rebel. Let's face it, I'm not built for revolution".

Still, he filled us with dissentious impulses. "I hope if there's one thing you learn from my class, it's to question everything—what others tell you, what you believe, your parents...especially your parents."

One of my early acts of rebellion was to smoke my first cigarette, a cheap Four Square, in a nook of Colaba. I was spotted by a classmate's parent, who informed Mini and Shivaji. Mini was amused. Everyone in her family smoked; I was simply following tradition. But

Shivaji, who considered smokers, especially women, degenerates, saw it as a moral failure and gave me an absurd lecture on "Indian values". He was reading the *Mahabbharata* at the time and tended to see everything in terms of a duel between good and evil.

"Maya, you have to stick to the right path. There are forces that will try to waylay you but you must be strong."

"Meaning what? All I did was smoke a cigarette."

"Today you smoked a cigarette, tomorrow you might do god knows what."

Karela's grand insurrection was to profile Parsis who would never make it to the anthologies of the illustrious. The rebels, but also the swindlers, charlatans, murderers. He told every batch about his project but, as far as I knew from the school alumni circuit, had done nothing about it.

"You never hear of Parsi cheats and killers but, let me tell you, there have been a few," he said.

I had to call him to learn about Bharucha. But first, I had to accompany Tumpa to an exhibition. After the financial crisis of 2008, the newspaper, fearing a dip in profits, axed the two arts pages to save the cost of newsprint. The arts section had been steadily eroded over the years. Five pages were cut to four, then to three, finally to two. Even when it turned out the crisis did no damage to the paper's bottomline, the pages weren't brought back. It was a show of the publisher's contempt for stuff that brought no advertising. Now the arts were covered only if big money was involved—say a painting sold at an auction for millions—or if the publisher's nephew, an ambitious but middling artist, was having a show. That day, Daniel Chacko, the resident editor, dispatched Tumpa to cover the guy's latest show, 'The Anatomy of Evanescence'.

The show had a bunch of video works and installations composed of 'found objects'. One video was of a bowl of fruit disintegrating over ten minutes, plump mangoes, peaches, apples and bananas infinitesimally rotting till they were blackened, putrefying lumps surrounded by a halo of flies. A composition of found objects—a passport picture of a boy, a chewed pencil stub, a toy helicopter that spun in the air if you yanked its cord, a torn Bata slipper, some buttons—was meant to suggest the longevity of objects compared to the fleeting nature of human life. In other words, the owner of the slipper might be dead but his footwear lived on, first on the street, now in a gallery and later, who knows, in a museum or the home of some collector. This foundling assortment was Kersi's Museum of Randomness right here.

"I want to know which dustbin he got all this shit from," Tumpa said.

Normally, I would've joined in Tumpa's disdain. So much of conceptual art was easy assemblage hinged on an ordinary idea. "Where's the workmanship, the skill?" Tumpa raved, angry that she'd have to do a puff job, an article in complimentary tones. But the work caused a constriction in my throat, reminding me of Burjor's box. He was dead, his things remained.

It was a day of omens. We saw that the gallery next door had an exhibition of photographs of Parsi bodybuilders. They'd been taken at an annual competition. Men with ripped, greased backs, boulders for arms, brick-like chests, clenched, solid butts. In one image, a grizzled old man, a veteran bodybuilder from the look of his physique, which had lost some definition with age, hung upside-down from a bar like a sleeping vampire. Naturally, I thought of the picture Burjor had enclosed of him lifting weights in a gym.

"Remember the physical culture story?" Tumpa said.

Some time back, we'd run a series of columns on Parsi arcana—why fire temple clocks are set thirty-eight minutes behind Indian Standard Time (because they run on Bombay Time, a colonial time zone), the only makers of close-toed slippers worn by priests (the Kerawallas in Dhobi Talao), the best place for sadras, kustis and other ritual items (Moolla and Sons on Princess Street), Parsi Hindustani classical musicians (the sitar player Keki Jijina and tabla player Aban Mistry). It was a popular series, judging by the number of letters and comments it got.

"If a Parsi sneezes it's news, bhenchod," Adi Sanjana, our volatile front-page editor, often said.

One of the columns was about Parsi gymnasiums in the early twentieth century. They had names like Gazdar's Health Home, Petit Gymnasium, the

Zoroastrian Physical Culture and Health League of Bombay, Daruwala's Health and Strength Club and they taught wrestling, swimming, badminton, bodybuilding. For some reason, skating was popular. The Bombay Skating Class at Gowalia Tank taught kids how to box, play badminton and do tricks on skates. Cycling was big too. In 1923, around thirty years before Burjor must have arrived in Bombay, six Parsi men from the Bombay Weightlifting Club set out to cycle around the world. Three dropped out along the way, three made it over four years and five months.

Back at work, I called Karela. He didn't remember me, even after I told him I was in Shalini Mirchandani's class. Every class has a few students who are more memorable than others. Shalini Mirchandani was the flag that marked my batch. Big boned with cloudy hair and an aura of self-assurance she seemed born with, Shalini was the spokesperson for our class, the negotiator, the troubleshooter. When petty classroom fights broke out, Shalini waded in to referee. The new maths teacher was a moron incapable of getting the class ready for the final board exams. Shalini led a delegation to the principal to complain. The teachers admired her statesman-like qualities. It was certain she was headed for a great career. I thought she was a bit of phony, fond of her image and studious about the friends she made. So I was pleased when she became an airhostess, baffling everyone.

"Were you the one with buck teeth?" Karela said on the phone.

"No," I said.

"The one who went prematurely grey?"

"No."

"You're the one who used to interchange your Vs and Ws. You'd say 'wovel' and 'vonderful'. It used to make me hysterical. Now that you're much older I can tell you that I preferred not to correct you because I found your habit so funny."

"That was Aditi."

I wasn't offended. I'll be the first to admit I was forgettable in school, lacking the personality, looks or grades that might set me apart. I wasn't a prankster like some, smearing absentminded Mr Dias's chair with chalk that would leave a white patch on the seat of his pants or trimming old Ms Desai's hair as she nodded off. Or, like Shalini, possessed of such poise as to pass off confidence as intelligence. This bothered me and I made efforts to develop a personality. Before the pottery and sushi rolling classes of adulthood, I tried things that were popular among schoolkids—elocution, tennis, drawing, even ballet, which I quit after watching a video of *Swan Lake* realizing I didn't have it in me to make it to the Bolshoi.

Karela agreed to meet me that week. Having retired early, he had little to do and by the eagerness in his voice, I sensed he was excited by this diversion.

16

Karela shares a flat with his sister at Oval Maidan. We sat in his living room, which speaks of old, family money. The rosewood sofas have backrests carved with thickets of leaves, the armoires have filigree doors, the tables are inlaid with floral, ceramic tiles, the glass cabinets are filled with crystal figurines, German silver and china. There are china dolls, cherubs, ballerinas, ball-gowned women holding parasols, baskets of fruit, sheep gambolling down a grassy slope. The walls have still lifes of flowers and fruit and oil paintings of Victorian women and children picnicking. The crowd of objects trapped light and seemed to obstruct the circulation of air in the room. There was the heavy stillness of a mausoleum.

Karela sat in the middle of the room on a worn leather chair draped with a printed rug at odds with the rest of the place. An aesthetic rebellion against the taste of his parents.

"These wooden sofas are fucking uncomfortable," he

said. "You can stop shifting, you're never going to get cosy on that thing."

Karela felt the need to explain the opulence of the apartment, how a retired schoolteacher could afford to live in a place this size without working. Breezily, but with apology clear in his tone, he told me his parents, both dead, had left him and his sister a hefty trust fund. The family had had an engineering business from colonial times; they used to make pumps and generators.

"I was the intellectual of the family," he said. "My folks were in awe of me and decided early on that I couldn't be expected to dirty my hands in business. I was meant for pursuits of the mind. So there was never any pressure to work. I could do whatever the fuck I wanted. Of course, they were disappointed that I chose to teach in a girls' school. They thought I'd go to Oxford or Cambridge and become a don or something. I told them that I needed a job that didn't tax me and gave me time to write books. And they bought it like they'd bought every claim I'd made in my life."

Karela was in striped shorts and a sleeveless sadra. I was seeing his legs and arms for the first time and it took some will power not to stare at the patch of grizzled chest hair the sadra exposed. He'd aged of course. His face had acquired furrows, lines and sagging folds. He still had a goatee; it was no longer sharp but limp like a much-used paintbrush. Yet, he was attractive and still capable, I imagined, of charming women of all ages.

"Now that I'm here, do you remember me?" I said.

"Vaguely. Which means you made little impression in school. But here you are, an editor in a big newspaper, asking questions about obscure, forgotten things. I'm impressed. Often, it's the ones you least expect that become successes. And the ones who show promise early on fizzle out. Look at me. I had the brains for a career in academia, maybe law. But I was lazy, indulged by my parents. You know I briefly dallied with the Communist Party, inspired by a fellow in college who belonged to a wealthy family. He joined the Naxals and went underground. He's going into my book of Parsi daredevils. That's what I do these days, write and research."

As we spoke, Karela's sister Zarine wandered in and out of the room, a wan figure in a floral nightie that ended mid-calf. Her face was lean like her brother's and creased with lapidary lines. She gave me a vacant smile and went about her business as if she wasn't really in this world.

"My sister Zarine had men flinging themselves at her like bugs at a lightbulb," Karela said. "We never came away from an event without her getting at least one marriage proposal. It became a joke in the family. But the men just weren't good enough; not one matched up to our father. He never approved of any of the guys either so that he'd have someone to nurse him when the arthritis got bad. So she waited and waited for the right guy till she lost her beauty and her mind."

"She can hear you."

"No, she can't. Zarine lives in her own solar system. Our dear departed father is the sun and she orbits him like a moon. To get her attention I have to speak very loudly. I think I taught you some Larkin in school? 'Whitsun Weddings' was it? The poem I should have done with you guys is 'This be the verse'. It starts: 'They fuck you up, your mum and dad'. But then I'd have had all your mums and dads at my throat. On the phone, when you told me about what you're looking for, I got the sense that you feel incomplete over not knowing your parents. Don't be. Because some parents are not worth knowing. More importantly, don't let not knowing stop you from doing things with your life."

"You just said you were impressed with how I've turned out."

"Let me deliver a sentence I would've no doubt written in your report card: 'There's room for improvement'. If you had real ambition, you'd be working at a better publication."

—

It was a day of judgement. Tumpa had earlier scolded me for complaining about my job. I'd whined about Daniel Chacko's fondness for inserting into the paper pictures of women in tiny clothes.

"You rant about your job but you do nothing to improve your situation. Which is why you've been at the paper for ten years. Ten years and you're still at your first job. You know what happens to people who stick around for that long here. Another five years and you'll become like Mallika, your brain will turn to vapour and escape from your ears."

Mallika had been an editor at the paper for twenty-five years. She used to be a journalist of some repute, covering rural poverty back when newspapers wrote about such things. But over the years, severe boredom and disillusionment had turned her into an infantile fifty-year-old. She only commissioned pieces on fluff like the latest wedding trends and Hindi soap operas and talked like a giddy teenager. To hear her squeal OMG! when she was excited was embarrassing. To become Mallika, was my greatest fear. The Hole, my constant companion, threatened to hoover me into its depths every time I spotted Mallika tittering girlishly over something stupid with the interns.

—

Karela handed me a slim monograph on Bharucha written by friends after he died. Once I'd leafed through it, he took it back, put it into a folder marked 'Burjorji Bharucha' and gave me a Xerox of the book.

"I have something else to show you," he said, opening his laptop.

The grainy black-and-white photograph showed eleven men, women and kids standing in line on the verandah of a house with a low, tiled roof. Behind them stood eleven priests tying kustis around the navjotees. They were all in white, the women in saris, the men in sadras and pajamas and the kids in sadras and shorts. Their faces were indistinct in the shadow of the verandah. I felt I'd been kicked in the gut. Karela didn't know when the picture was taken, whether it was of the 1942 navjote or one of the several ceremonies that took place in the following years. Could Burjor be one of the kids in the picture? I was powerfully stirred by the spirit of the event, the daring of a few men to stage this rebellion when they knew the consequences would be fierce. Karela said the Parsis of Bombay, who've always been more orthodox than Parsis in other towns and cities, were outraged. There were scathing editorials, furious petitions.

Before I left with the photocopied monograph, Karela instructed me to call him with updates. He was interested in Homi Sukhadia's narrative on Burjor.

"You've come at the right time. My book is nearly done."

"I've been hearing about this book for twenty years."

"And you will soon see it in print. I've got a title, 'The Parsi Pirate: Stories of Rebels and Unsung Heroes'."

That night, Mini and I shared a joint rolled with luminously green marijuana that Kersi had acquired from a dealer who had arrived from Kerala. I had been filling her in on my conversation with Homi uncle. Then, pleasantly euphoric, comfortable in bed in my grotto of cushions, I read about Burjorji Bharucha's life. He was, by this account, a ballsy, complex character, deeply religious and conservative in many ways yet forward thinking. A pal of Gandhi and Nehru, he sold khadi door to door. He was sentenced to jail by the Surat court for organizing a march at dawn of nationalists singing patriotic songs. (The Bombay High Court overruled Surat.) In 1921, he joined a protest against the Prince of Wales's visit. Unlike his pro-British brethren, who went to welcome the Prince and got mobbed by the nationalists. That year, he quit a well-paying job in the state accountancy to do social work full time—running sewing classes for women in Navsari and Bombay so that they could fend for themselves, organizing English tutorials for Parsi kids in Udvada, contributing money towards a library in the town.

The tall, light-eyed Bharucha—he was described thus by Karela, whose mother had learned to sew at his class in Navsari—could've lived comfortably. Instead he chose a monkish life, inspired perhaps by Gandhi. He slept on a trunk in a modest room in Fort. He wrote letters on waste paper. He was vegetarian and took his meals in a cheap joint close to his home. That night, I had a dream in which Bharucha and visions of 'Kubla Khan', which Karela had taught us in school, were stitched together. Bharucha, a Christ-like figure in a dagli and prayer cap with flashing eyes and floating hair, flying through a cavernous landscape.

17

It was the middle of March 2009, which meant Navroze was coming up. Every year, the paper ran a picture of a Parsi celebrity posing before a table of food and a story on Parsi colonies. Every year Daniel Chacko, the head of the bureau, suggested the story as if it had just occurred to him. Like Mallika, the fifty-going-on-fifteen editor, Chacko should have moved on a decade ago.

Tall, wiry, Chacko moved with the grace of a Malyali toddy tapper and had a strong, angular face that would've fit right into a Soviet propaganda poster. He was popular with women, though not entirely because of his looks. Even though he rarely had a good idea and needlessly published racy pictures of Hindi movie stars, there was no denying the man was smart. Having a conversation with him was thrilling; his knowledge of history and politics was vast and he had the intellect to yoke together diverse ideas. He was an intellectual ape, capable of swinging in a single conversation from the reorganization of Indian states along linguistic lines after Independence to dying aboriginal languages to rebellions in the North- East. I heard his idea of foreplay was walking his dates around the older parts of Bombay and plying them with local history. Apparently, his favourite routine was a stroll around Lalbaug. He'd take his dates to the area's many unusual temples, point out the spectacular sixth-century statue of a seven-headed Shiva, perambulate past the shells of textile mills, shepherd them to chivda galli to buy and snack on fried foods and thus demonstrate his street cred. Throughout he'd keep up a running commentary on the area's history. It was a shtick he'd repeated several times since the relationships never lasted, being as frivolous at love as he was with work.

"He sounds like you," Tumpa had once said.

I'd once bumped into him at Kala Ghoda on a Sunday. He was with a much younger girl outside David Sassoon Library, taking her on the Bombay neo-Gothic strip tour no doubt. I happened to dart out from the pavement of Elphinstone College at the exact moment Chacko reached an arm around her waist and gave it a squeeze. On seeing me, smirking as I advanced, he pulled away in embarrassment. The next minute, slow moving Kersi emerged from the vaulted pavement. We'd just finished lunch at New Martin's and were bound for Kala Ghoda for coffee and dessert. "Babe," Kersi called out, suggesting to Chacko that we were a couple. At work, I was known to be single. Now it was Chacko's turn to smirk. In the spirit of hospitality, or to show to his new paramour his generosity as a boss, Chacko insisted we all have coffee.

We walked towards Kala Ghoda Café; Chacko amused the girl by cracking jokes at my expense.

"The first time I met Maya, I put her down as the kind of girl with whom you have to be careful about what you say. She doesn't talk much, she smiles even less. You know me, I'm a funny guy, I like to make, what we used to call as kids, non-veg jokes, pull a fast one now and then. I thought this girl is one of those earnest chicks who would run to HR to complain of sexual harassment at the slightest gag."

"His idea of a joke," I said to the girl, "is telling a woman about to get married that she better lose five kilos quick or she might smother her husband to death on their wedding night. Or telling a pretty, young reporter that she'll go far while openly appraising her and winking at one of his cronies."

"Fuck you Maya, I didn't mean anything. It's just harmless goofery."

"Classic misogynist response."

"Don't listen to Maya. She's bitter like a bad cucumber and destined to die alone."

"See what I mean."

There had been a brief squaring up between Chacko and Kersi, as is often the case when men meet each other for the first time. Chacko had triumphed in the subliminal contest. He'd gauged that while Kersi is an attractive guy, he's of inferior intellect. He understood this from Kersi's drawl, protracted by years of smoking pot, his inability to participate in the conversation, which hopped from city history to current affairs to his own subject, yoga. Smarting from being exposed before his date, Chacko made an extra effort to put Kersi down. When the conversation wound its way to yoga, sweet Kersi, thinking he could finally contribute, said with gusto that yoga went back thousands of years only to be interrupted by Chacko, who with smirking pedantry pointed out that the rishis might have sat in lotus poses and practiced some basic bodily contortions for years but modern yoga, as we know it, was largely a twentieth century phenomenon. I felt defensive, wanting to point out that Kersi might not be an intellectual but he had a practical intelligence. He was resourceful, the kind of person you turned to in a time of crisis. Moreover, he wasn't a phony like Chacko, a yes man masquerading as a revolutionary. His heart bled for the poor—struggling former textile mill workers, suicidal farmers. Yet, he buried their stories in the middle and back pages in favour of articles on flats being sold for terrific sums, the craze for speedboats among the wealthy. He liked to rail against anyone living in south Bombay.

"You know where I was during 26/7?" he said over coffee. The ricocheting bumper car of our conversation had hit the flood of 2005. "Walking in waist-deep water, from Fort to Borivali. I waded through shit, piss and muck while you were dry as toast."

"I was dry because I was in office till one in the morning editing copy your reporters handed in way past deadline," I said.

"Whatever. Up north there's no drainage, there are no pavements. It's a fucking jungle. You townies won't last a day."

The truth was that Chacko was embarrassed of his privilege. His father, a well-paid corporate executive, had made enough to buy his only son a flat. Every year, he earned fat bonuses and a couple of years ago, the poverty-loving boy from IC Colony in Borivali had bought a Mercedes. Every time one of us brought it up—we got a kick out of seeing him squirm—he stressed it was second-hand.

"Luckily, he doesn't have to walk on pavements," I said to the girl. "He drives around in a Mercedes." Chacko frowned, the girl looked at him with raised eyebrows. He must've spun an apocryphal yarn about taking the train every day.

Once again Chacko suggested we profile a handful of Parsi colonies in time for the new year. He wanted to do things differently. Instead of two hundred words on five colonies, he suggested a series of largish profiles to be run through the week. The story of each colony was to be told through the lens of a charismatic resident. (He promised a thousand words but I knew from experience it would be trimmed to seven hundred to make place for something silly or an ad.) I signed up to write about Naval Baug, with the thought of seeing the colony where Burjor had lived and meeting Hilla and Jimmy Kapadia, whose names were listed in his letter.

18

Naval Baug sits in a narrow lane in Lalbaug, its pale, yellow buildings like blocks of butter. There was a sense of entering a sub universe with its own atmosphere and modes of being. I felt like an interloper, the feeling compounded when, two sadra-clad men polishing a bike, father and son from the look of them, on seeing my hesitant advance asked with polite suspicion where I was headed. Then they pointed me to the building where the Kapadias lived, a chawl-like structure with common balconies like most of the blocks in the colony.

I had called beforehand to explain my dual purpose. They'd been thrilled to finally fulfil the request Burjor had made years ago to tell his daughter about her father—and to be featured in a major newspaper. In their seventies, they lived in a two-room flat. The carpet-sized living room was dominated by a display case full of crockery marking the marriage of Charles and Diana, delicate cups and saucers, dessert plates, a teapot, all bearing portraits of the royal couple. In between were black-and-white pictures of Jimmy and Hilla when they were young—in costume in a play, dancing, he in a dagli, she in a polka-dotted dress. They'd both been clerks in a bank. In the evenings, they'd perform in plays and revues by Adi Marzban, the Parsi-Gujarati playwright famous for his dexterity with words. Even though his oeuvre was limited, by and large, to bedroom comedy. They'd been a good looking couple, he lean and nimble with a slim moustache and Dev Anand hair, she slim, delicate with a stylish bob and dramatically painted eyes.

"We can do the jive, foxtrot, cha-cha-cha, any ballroom dance. You name it," Jimmy said.

"Let's show her Jimmy," Hilla said.

The two jumped up and did a silent jive for a couple of minutes. It was touching to watch them, laced with wrinkles, losing shape with age, swing each other around cautiously so as not to dislocate an elbow or fall over and bust a hip. Once the performance was over, they gave me chai and khari biscuits smeared with strawberry jam and told me about Burjor.

Burjor moved into Naval Baug in the early seventies when Hilla and Jimmy were twenty-something neighbours conducting a clandestine affair. Hilla had been promised by her father to Phiroze who, upon passing his chartered accountancy exam, was sure to get a good job. Jimmy, in comparison, was just a commerce graduate. Romantic rivalries were common in Naval Baug, often resulting in fistfights. Phiroze, a hot-headed fellow, took it for granted that Hilla was his even though she had told him that, despite her father's promise, she would only marry Jimmy. He acted like a boyfriend, showing up at the bank where she worked to fetch her in the evenings, sending her flowers. So when Phiroze, who dove into fights with the same anticipation of pleasure as one plunging into an inviting water body, who was the leader of a band of boys whose evenings were spent in the compound name-calling the colony's eccentrics and mentally challenged individuals, whose own mother was afraid of her son's lightening flares of anger, found Hilla sitting on Jimmy's lap in a dark corner of the building stairwell, he lost his mind. He dragged Jimmy to the common balcony and began to pummel his skinny rival with brutish fists. Meanwhile, Hilla screamed for help bringing people to their doors and windows. The only one to answer her call was Burjor, who had run out of his flat to the balcony in the building across. He sprinted down the stairs, crossed the compound, ran up the stairs of Hilla's building and, reaching the embattled twosome—Phiroze was pulping Jimmy's face as if it were a large, soft fruit—he yanked Phiroze by the shoulders and threw him against the wall.

"Your father was a big guy," Jimmy said. "Phiroze was short but strong. One was a pole, one was a barrel."

As Burjor and Phiroze used to work out at the same gym across the colony, they each had a measure of the other's strength. But whereas Burjor, who had a bit of boxing training, knew how to parry punches, Phiroze attacked with the mindless force displayed by those possessing the deadly combination of a quick temper and extreme stupidity. Finally, his face purple, his nose bloodied, Phiroze was led away by his father, himself a legendary bully in his youth.

"That day was the start of our friendship. And when Hilla and I wanted to do hanky-panky, we would go to Burjor's house. He lived alone, you see, and was out most of the day."

At the time, Burjor drove a cab, first a Hillman Minx, then a Fiat. In his spare time, he'd hit the gym meant only for Parsis, just outside the colony. This was where the colony's amateur bodybuilders worked out, accordioning the air with push-ups, sit-ups, the swinging of weights. One of the musclemen, Faram, would put on a show every year at the colony's annual hill station retreat. At night after dinner, Faram would oil his body and, emerging in his underpants, perform bodybuilding manoeuvres before a whistling audience, his muscles gleaming in the radiance of strategically placed lamps.

In the gym, Burjor was respected by his peers for being able to do a record number of push-ups. It was a good thing for his mysterious origins—no one knew anything about his family—and his toffee-coloured skin would normally have made him a colony punching bag, like the cripples and mentally disabled.

"It's a myth that all Parsis are fair. We've been here so long, the sun has baked us properly. But with Burjor, you knew there was some mixture. His features were Parsi but the skin was darker than usual," Hilla said.

In private, they called him dubra, a nasty epithet applied to dark-hued Parsis suspected of having alien blood. But never to his face—until the bust-up with Phiroze, who would afterwards, sotto voce, utter the word when the two crossed paths in the gym.

In general, Burjor, a quiet sort, aloof from the matrix of colony life, was left alone. He was considered a useful person, being a taxi driver. Someone who could, in an emergency, be called upon to drive people places. He would often drive Jimmy and Hilla, after they were married and could be seen together safely, to rehearsal. The two sang in Adi Marzban's revues and acted in his comedies. He would watch them rehearse and occasionally pitch in backstage. Burjor might not have known at the time the conservative line taken by the paper Marzban edited on the navjote of 1942, the stinging editorials on letting kids of mixed blood into the Zoroastrian fold.

"Did you guys know about his 'dubra' blood?" I asked.

"We did," Jimmy said. "Others found out. There were consequences. But we'll come to that later."

Burjor began to get noticed when it was clear he was no longer a struggling taxi driver. There were signs of money coming in, though he tried to be subtle. The first sign was the news that he owned a carpet, at the time an object of luxury. Every Sunday, the colony's kids went door to door to collect old newspapers. These were sold to raise money for the Baug's cultural and sporting activities. One lad reported seeing, what seemed to his eyes, a plush carpet, rich with ethnic design, the kind he'd seen in magazine advertisements. Word spread and folks wondered how a taxi driver had afforded a carpet.

He began wearing shoes whereas earlier he'd worn cheap chappals. A greater variety in his clothing was observed. No longer did he alternate between three shirts and two pairs of trousers. Since he had been working out, the clothes fit better.

"How do you think Burjor could afford nice clothes and a carpet?" I asked.

"He never talked about work but I know he was involved in smuggling," Jimmy said. "I remember in the seventies he used to wear a fancy watch. What was it called?"

"Ricoh?"

"Yes, could be. Anything that was flashy or expensive-looking was smuggled back then."

"The other thing people realized was that Burjor was a good-looking guy," Hilla said. "Especially the ladies."

A practice of name-calling existed in the colony. Anyone with a peculiarity, physical or behavioural, was given a mean cognomen by the bullies. Ardeshir Anklesaria, a trade unionist at a Lalbaug mill where he worked as a supervisor, was called Langdo Lal. Langdo because he had a limp, a consequence of polio at a young age, and Lal, red, because he was a Communist. Kavas Marolia, a hulking thirty-year-old with the brain of a child, was labelled Gando, the demented. Kavas would spend his days sitting on a stool outside his flat. Little kids, steeped in silly horrors by their parents, would fear to cross his path imagining he'd grab them and crush them with his considerable arms. Burjor, aside from being surreptitiously called dubra by Phiroze and his cronies, was generally nameless till he drew the attention of Naval Baug's women.

Girls from white-collar families that would never stand for their daughters associating with a cabbie watched jealously as working class girls stopped Burjor in the compound for a flirtatious word or contrived to ring his doorbell. One woman, however, had no objection to Burjor's station. Hufrish Desai looked like a fifties Hollywood starlet with her big black eyes and big hair that she spent much time arranging in a cataract of curls. Every man in the colony lusted after her—"Except my Jimmy," Hilla interjected—and, simultaneously, disparaged her for being a femme fatale. This was untrue, a convenient construction hinged on three things. Hufrish was friendly, comfortable being the only woman in male company unlike other, more timid girls, which led men to assume she was easy. Men, both married and single, repeatedly propositioned her. She ignored them leading them to believe she was a tease. And it was well known that her husband Pesi Desai, an optician, had erectile trouble, which meant she must be desperate for sex. Poor Pesi was called Puchhu Keru, soft banana. If Phiroze and his band of louts happened to be prowling the compound in the evening when Hufrish returned from work, they would, on seeing her, start a low, ape-like chant, "Huf, huf, huf, huf..." She was secretary to a chairman in a big company and it was assumed, naturally, that she was sleeping with the boss.

Burjor and Hufrish had a scene that lasted some months. Sensing he was mature enough to handle an affair and keep it discrete, she made a move.

"What was the move?" I asked.

"That only Hufrish knows," Jimmy said. "She and Pesi migrated to Canada many years ago."

It was tough to keep things quiet in a place like Naval Baug, where everyone could see who crossed the common balconies to enter whose flat. They tried to keep their assignations at times when half the colony had gone to work and the other half was inside, away from the heat. They communicated through Jermai, an old woman who lived in the widows' chawl. She scratched a living doing odd jobs like delivering pouches of milk from the booth outside the colony to people's doorsteps. As Burjor and Hufrish's courier, she earned a few rupees. But who knows, she could well have been the tattler, for perpetual desperation had made her a wily fox. After their affair became well known, Burjor was given the sobriquet Burjor Bairi-chor, Burjor the wife stealer, by the colony's name-calling committee, namely Phiroze and his goons. Pesi himself had no objection, or if he did he kept a gentlemanly silence out of guilt. Hufrish, in her thirties, her sexual prime, should not have to be celibate because of him. Pesi's grace was even more scandalous than Hufrish's affair. It was too modern for the time. And so Pesi was given a second name by Phiroze and his posse of brutes, Bakro, goat, his wife's fool.

None of this seriously bothered Burjor, who seemed to waft in his own sphere, removed from the earthly pettiness of Naval Baug. This aloofness, the sense that his atmosphere was naturally insulated from the emotional tempests of the world, bothered Hufrish, who made the mistake of hoping their affair would go somewhere. She confided in Hilla. The affair didn't stop Burjor from responding to overtures by girls in the colony (nothing more than flirty chatter), but outside, he played the field.

"He was your father but don't get me wrong when I say he was a haraami when it came to women," Jimmy said, punching me on the arm. "Guy broke a lot of hearts."

One of the hearts belonged to Philomena, a Goan Catholic girl from Dhobi Talao. Completely off the mark in her assessment of Burjor, Philomena—Philly to her friends and family—dreamt of marrying the man. When it was clear Burjor was not the marrying kind, she showed up at the colony to deliver comeuppance. Banging her delicate fists on his door—I was told she was slightly built with a shapely figure she wrapped in tight dresses—Philly called Burjor a "bleddy bastard of the first order", "a scoundrel with a capital 'S'", a sinner whom Jesus Christ would never forgive". Her outburst brought the colony to the compound and balconies. Phiroze and his beastly boys were delighted and briefly took to calling Burjor Macapao, the slang for pao-eating Goans. Hufrish didn't see him for weeks after the showdown.

"To be honest, we were all a little jealous of Burjor," Jimmy said. "He was getting all the action...I mean not me. I had Hilla."

Hilla had it from Hufrish that Burjor never made his intentions explicit. He never said that he was only interested in a casual liaison, nothing more. When they were together, he was generous, thoughtful, husband-like. Yet, he carried on with other women, which baffled and pained Hufrish.

"Basically, he sent wrong signals," Hilla said.

After Philomena, there was a long lull in Burjor's love life. At least, there was no public drama. This was the time, I calculated, when unbeknown to Homi, Hilla and Jimmy, Burjor and Mini were conducting their shy romance. He drove the cab less and, in the colony, he received all sorts of people, mostly men but there were women too.

"Who were they?" I asked.

Initially Hilla and Jimmy assumed they were fellow smugglers and began to keep their distance fearing "god know what hera pheri he was up to". Till Armaity entered Burjor's life.

19

As I'd predicted my profile of Naval Baug told through the story of Hilla and Jimmy was axed from eight hundred to five hundred words. Despite his promise that the Baug series would be prominently displayed, Chacko inserted a large ad on the very page my piece was carried, which meant all the stories, except the ones on thefts and murders, had to be trimmed. Normally, this would have thrown me into a paroxysm of self-pity. What was I doing at this rag? Why had I wasted my brain for ten years? What was stopping me from leaving this place? Nothing, Sartre would've said. I was free to quit and get a better job. But that in itself was the problem, the anguish of freedom, the fact that I had the choice. I would've called Tumpa to discuss my departure, she would enthusiastically list my options and I would, encouraged by my bright future, declare that this year would be my last. But both of us knew I wasn't going to leave a gig so cushy it was compared to government jobs. This time, however, my mind was distracted by Burjor's story.

I had a rapt audience in Mini, Kersi, Tumpa and Karela. I was excited by their curiosity and steady attention and was euphoric that for the first time, I had stories to tell other than tales from Bombay's history. According to Tumpa, I was looking better, radiant with an inner blaze.

To Mini, I would narrate the annals of Burjor at night over a post-prandial spliff in the balcony overlooking the lambent Colaba street. She would, no doubt, pass on what she'd learned to Shivaji. To Kersi, I would report over a post-coital doobie. In fact, I'd noticed he'd been coming on to me more than usual. Kersi, a Luddite without a smartphone, who took five minutes to tap out a short message, had begun sending me flirty texts during the day. Now he didn't have a way with words, a lack of reading and long exposure to drugs having limited his range of expression. Yet, the brutish brevity of his texts had an effect. After wrapping up at the paper, I was so worked up, we often ended up having sex. (Conveniently, his room had its own entrance.) Who would've thought this new development would make me more attractive to men?

"What a player Burjor was," Kersi said, pausing before adding, "like you."

"What do you mean?"

It turned out that Kersi had read a text on my phone from Mao. It was a sorrowful message about our fantastic night together and how he wished it wasn't our last.

In keeping with the skein of duality that runs through my life, my other occasional lover was a Bengali business executive. He had an unfortunate name, Shagnik Das. Everyone knew him by either of two nicknames, Shaggy or Mao, the latter given by parents who, when young, were in the thick of the Naxalite movement. The name was a homage to the Great Leader.

We met at a film festival screening. I was reading *Humboldt's Gift*, waiting for the film to begin, when Mao took the neighbouring seat.

"I feel like Charlie Citrine these days," he said. "I want a divorce, but she won't give me one till I sell my flat and pay her half the proceeds."

"Is she fifteen years younger and a floozy?"

"Five."

Things between us ended after a year. Mao wanted to go steady but I didn't. He said it was best to sever things instead of risking deeper emotional involvement. He'd been through one trial with his marriage, he didn't have the stamina for another.

"You're the guy in this," he said.

Now for the second time in my life, my romantic outlook was being compared to that of Burjor.

"Are you saying I'm a slut?" I said to Kersi with hostility.

"No babe, I'm just jealous I guess," he said, with such feeling in his eyes I had to turn away.

Kersi's comment did, however, seed a smidge of doubt. Was my detachment towards men congenital?

Why did I not actively seek meaningful relationships? Wasn't it a strange contradiction—I liked feeling tethered to the city but I did nothing about finding an anchor in a partner? What was I waiting for?

"The right guy," said Tumpa, when I put the questions to her. "I mean, look at the candidates. Kersi is sweet but the drugs have vaporized half his brain. He talks at the speed of someone walking through sand. And Mao is such a dandy. You can't be with a man who wears bow-ties and collects canes."

"He doesn't collect canes."

"Whatever. Money has made him poncey. The point is you're just a horny girl. Nothing wrong with that."

"I'm in my thirties, at my sexual peak, of course I'm horny. I can't contain my hormones, they're coming out of every goddamn orifice. But jokes aside, what if I'm incapable of love?"

"Don't be dramatic, you're not really Bengali. Just hang in there for Mr Right, who may—or may not—come along."

Mini had figured out about Kersi. She disapproved of my friendship, as she quaintly put it, believing teaching yoga was a frivolous occupation. She would've preferred Mao, a man with a conservative job.

"Since you're not doing much with your life, at least find a guy with whom you can have a meaningful relationship," she said, with the effortless cruelty of parents.

"Like all parents, you want me to get married, have

babies and be miserable to show I'm an adult. For all your liberal values, you're a conservative just like Shivaji."

"Twenty years later you're going to wake up one morning realizing that you've made no impression on the world, left no trace except countless joint butts. Don't say I didn't warn you."

I didn't need any more warnings. They were all around me. My own anxieties inclined me to weigh daily observations with semiotic importance. A mini anchor at the Yacht Club brought to mind a comparison with an unmoored ship; slippers a few inches away from the wall spoke of a lack of ambition, the wall becoming a finish line out of reach; a half-eaten biscuit became a sign of an incomplete life.

But I digress. I meant to continue with Burjor and Armaity's story, which I learned over the course of several visits. She lived with her old aunt and uncle, having been orphaned at a young age. Like Burjor, she was keen on fitness. As a kid, she'd gone to a class at Gowalia Tank at which children were taught to skate. Her specialty was trick skating—she could do backbends and pirouettes on skates and even play a tune on the violin while making lemniscates with her wheels. She was so attached to her roller skates that she'd wheel around the house in them. Jimmy, who knew her uncle recalled visiting their place and being served tea by a roving Armaity.

"Her balance was perfect. She held the tray with a teacup with just one hand," Jimmy said.

As an adult, she joined the gym across the colony, the same one visited by Burjor, where she was known for her gymnastic feats. Still she went unnoticed till she turned twenty-one. That year, the puppy fat on her face melted, revealing strong cheekbones and a delicate jaw. The youthful acne vanished from the marble of her skin and her black hair seemed darker, more lustrous. Overnight, she began to be noticed by boys, who had till then barely registered her presence.

"Her mother was Irani," Hilla explained. "They've had fewer centuries in the Indian sun."

From a young age, she'd learned to sew at classes run by Burjorji Bharucha nearby. To support her uncle and aunt, she dropped out of college to work as a seamstress with a woman near the colony, who tailored clothes. An expert cutter, especially of dresses that were in vogue at the time, Armaity was sought by the colony's fashionable ladies. Before Armaity became a challenger, Hufrish commissioned her to make several dresses. She was particularly fond of the shirt-dress that fit snugly over her admirable breasts and flared out in a whorl of pleats that skimmed her hips.

One of the colony fellows to seriously pursue Armaity was Cyrus Mehta. Handsome, well-built, Cyrus worked as a mechanic in a typewriter factory. He was a self-taught engineer, a genius with gadgets and motorbikes. On weekends, he could be seen tending to his beloved Yezdi in trousers and sadra. Till the day his father, Boman, a drunk and a gambler, sold it to pay off his debts. That day, father and son nearly came to blows on the balcony outside their home.

"Remember the name," Jimmy said.

Cyrus ran with Phiroze and his swinish crew. Sweet and dutiful as a child, Cyrus became hardened after his mother died and he was raised by Boman, who did only one thing with any regularity—beat the kid for no good reason. In general with women, he was fickle. But with Armaity, things were different. Perhaps he saw in her something of his mother's kindness and childlike openness for he was disarmed. But Armaity had seen Cyrus taunt and play pranks on the colony's mentally challenged folks and believed he was beyond reform. She rebuffed him and then enraged him by gravitating towards Burjor, the colony's apex paramour.

One day, Armaity's uncle had a seizure, collapsing as spasms rippled through his frail body. She rang Burjor's doorbell, like many had in times of emergency, and asked him to take them to the hospital. The old man made it. (He and his wife would die within a week of each other some months down the line.) Burjor, noticing Armaity's fresh-faced beauty that would only increase with time, began to court her, applying his successful technique of alternating charm and avuncular concern with aloof withdrawal. He'd be the attentive lover one day and not call or meet for the next three. It confused women yet fanned the cinders of curiosity.

"Wait a second, how do you know this?" I asked.

"Armaity used to confide in me," Hilla said. "He did this hot-cold thing very well."

Perhaps out of gratitude, Armaity relaxed her wary shield, which she had deployed with Cyrus, and submitted to him. Naturally, Cyrus, who had hated Burjor since the episode with Phiroze and who was jealous of his sway over women, was outraged. He was hurt that Armaity had sought Burjor's help, ignoring the practicality of it. Burjor had a cab; Cyrus had a bike. Together with his cronies, Cyrus took revenge. They did this by attacking Burjor's cab, deflating the tyres one night, snipping wires, smashing headlights. Naturally, Cyrus was caught. In the contest, Burjor demolished his face. A drunk Boman wavered into the scene and for once taking up for his son, swore payback. Poor Armaity, feeling responsible for Cyrus's roguery, drew closer to Burjor.

"Bugger should have left her alone," Jimmy said. "He was eleven years older."

Not long after the bust-up with Cyrus, two things happened. Armaity's uncle and aunt passed, he of a heart attack, she, out of shock and sadness, leaving the girl more vulnerable than ever. Usually, careful when it came to sex, Burjor managed to knock Armaity up. They had to get married. Naturally, she was thrilled. She needed an anchor and what better person than a fit, handsome, older and wiser man? Burjor, on the other hand, felt snared in a trap of his own making. Desperate for a way out, he sought counsel from Jimmy and Hilla.

"I told him straight. You've dug your grave, now you lie in it. If you're half a man, you'll marry her without a second thought. And for god's sake be good to the girl," Jimmy said.

There was no wedding. Just a visit to the marriage registrar's office at Old Custom House in Ballard Estate to sign papers with Jimmy and Hilla as witnesses. Afterwards, they walked down to Hamilton Studios to get portraits taken. The picture Burjor had left me was taken there. He was in a brown suit standing as she, in a pale pink sari pinned at her left shoulder with a rosette, the nacreous broach nesting in my inherited carton, sat on a chair. Armaity was happy, though, attentive to her new husband's signs and signals, she knew he was upset. Burjor tried to be jovial but would, ever so often, fall into a pensive mood. Back in the colony the following day, they celebrated with a few friends, neighbours and a couple of Burjor's mysterious colleagues over dinner. Jimmy investigated for signs of smuggled goods—electronics, bolts of material, cabinets of booze. But Burjor's place looked any other Naval Baug home. There was no carpet even. The fancy stuff must be hidden in cupboards, Jimmy thought. Armaity cooked a terrific meal of kheema kebabs, saans ni machhi, mutton pulao and caramel custard. That day she wore a navy sari with an ivory border of birds in foliage. At last, after dessert, Burjor delighted Jimmy by bringing out a bottle of Scotch.

20

Excited by the progress of my pursuit, I began searching for Imelda Braganza immediately after my first meeting with Hilla and Jimmy.

Finding her was a workout. She no longer lived at the address in Dhobi Talao which Burjor had given. I went to a few homes on the street but got no answers. It turned out that Imelda was a fighter. After scrapping with her neighbours for years, she had no friends in the area. All they knew was that she had moved to Santa Cruz to live with her sister. She had no cellphone either. Occasionally, she'd be seen at the parish church for Sunday service. Why not ask the father if he knew? But the priest was a new fellow, who said he'd need a few days to check whether the office had Imelda's new address. After a morning of going door-to-door, listening to old ladies say "what you want to find that fighter cock for?" and "tell her she borrowed my steel dabba and didn't give it back", I bought a packet of garlic sticks at Paris Bakery, down the road from Our Lady of Dolours Church. Nibbling on a buttery finger,

I decided to try the neighbouring butcher shop, an establishment veiled with flanks of pig. Inside, a man was breaking down a leg of pork on his block. Did he know Imelda? Ya, he said, sundering a joint with his cleaver. Did he know where in Santa Cruz she lived? Near Kalina market, in a building bang opposite the mosque.

I scoped out three buildings across the mosque. These were middle-class societies that cared moderately about security, which meant the watchman was an old fellow who could be easily convinced to let you upstairs to ring every doorbell. At the third building, I heard Imelda before spotting her as I walked up the stairs. She was rowing loudly with Mrs Peters, who lived in the flat just above hers. The issue was a leaking toilet that was causing water to seep into the walls of Imelda's bathroom. Naturally loud, the voice boomed in the echo chamber of the stairwell. There was anger in that voice, not just over the leaking toilet, but a subcutaneous lava roiled by years of repeated disappointment. I was about to meet the Catholic version of Ratna.

When I rounded the stairs, I was startled to see a woman at odds with the voice. I'd assumed a voice like that would need a substantial receptacle, that she'd be a big woman. But like Ratna, Imelda was reed-thin. Unlike Ratna, she had an attractive face which, in a state of repose, radiated a sense of monkish serenity. Nothing about the face suggested an inflammable object.

"You're Imelda, yes?" I said, suddenly nervous before

her hostile gaze. "Hello, I'm Maya, Burjor's daughter."

"Ya, you got his Pinocchio nose. Are you a liar also, haan? Come inside. Peters, fix the toilet or I'll fix you."

She lived with her older sister Loretta, a sweeter facsimile suffering dementia. Loretta was watching TV in the living room when I entered. Had she seen me before? My face looked familiar. Did I work the ticket counter at Santa Cruz station?

"You've not been to the station in years boss," Imelda said. "She steps out twice a year, Easter and Christmas mass."

I sat with Loretta as Imelda vanished into the kitchen and began to make hospitable noises, water being heated, plates coming off the rack, which meant I was going to be there for a while. Loretta was pleased to have a distraction. She smiled a lot and had the same faraway look in her eyes as Karela's sister as if she was both present and not. She asked where I'd got such pretty flowers from.

"What flowers?"

"The lilies on your head, dear."

"She sees things," Imelda shouted from the kitchen. Loretta beamed, stroked my hand. "One day it's roses, next day it's marigold. Yesterday, she saw crocuses. I don't know how she knows what a crocus looks like. I had to ask a friend, what the hell is a crocus. Must be that Discovery channel she watches."

"So fresh, sweet smelling," Loretta cooed.

"What an actor. She has a cold and she can smell

lilies," Imelda said, setting down a tray with a pot of tea, a plate of meatloaf sandwiches and slices of plum cake, both of which she made to order.

"I had to do something when the daru business was finished," she said.

"How did you know I'm crazy about meatloaf?"

"I make it all the time, my clothes, my hair smell of the stuff. I took care of you when you were little. Somewhere in your baby brain, the smell must have registered it seems."

"You said Burjor was a liar?"

"Loretta, go inside. I have to talk to Maya about some private stuff," Imelda commanded. Loretta, still smiling, rose and glided indoors on the float of her floral nightie.

"What goes in through her ears, you never know how it will come out of her crazy brain. She and Peters are best friends, they love to do ghus-pus about me."

Philomena, Philly, Burjor's ex-girlfriend who created a scene when she realized things were going nowhere with the guy, was Imelda's daughter. The two of them had been carrying on for some time even though Imelda had warned Philly that Burjor was a Don Juan, a good man in general, but a cad when it came to women.

"She was *your* daughter! Jesus!"

"No one could have helped her, not even our Lord. She was weak, stupid and boy crazy. And stubborn for no reason. I told Burjor, 'Stay away from her.' He said 'Yes, yes' but went behind my back, bhenchod. Sorry girlie, he was your father and I loved him like a son. But in this respect, he was rascal."

After it ended—this was towards the mid-seventies—Philomena married the first suitor who came along. Augustine D'Souza, a civil engineer, proposed two months after they began dating. They married and migrated to Canada soon after. I noticed a framed picture of them on a cabinet in the room. Philly, a younger version of Imelda in a gauzy dress with giant mutton-chop sleeves, and Augustine, in a loud three-piece suit, a helmet of hair hugging his small face. Philomena couldn't get away fast enough, from Bombay, where her one true love lived and serially wooed women, and from her mother, to whom she'd transferred the blame of her failed relationship with Burjor.

"She hates me because I was right," Imelda said.

And because Imelda refused to cut ties with Burjor after the break-up. "I told her, if I stop working with Burjor, what will we eat? He's our bread and butter. But she only thought about her own misery. She was useless at life, like her father."

In the seventies, at the time of Prohibition, Imelda ran a clandestine bar from her home in Dhobi Talao. An 'aunty bar', the kind Thomas D'Mello, the newsroom's blind clairvoyant had told me about at the office party. Burjor and his colleague, Madhu Pereira, would supply hooch made in the bogs of the city's suburbs, the cheap distillate of rotting fruit, to bars like Imelda's. They'd drive their cabs out to Andheri and Vasai and return with the contraband hidden in tyres. Imelda's bar was a two-table affair in her living room. A lookout was posted on the balcony. The cops were paid off, which meant most nights were peaceful. But sometimes they swooped down on bars in surprise raids. When the lookout sounded an alarm, patrons would be herded out of the living room into the kitchen from where a staircase wound down to the ground floor below.

"Your father was pally with the cops. He was a talker, he could patao anyone—girls, cops, you name it," Imelda said.

After some years of selling hooch, Burjor moved on to bigger game. As Hilla and Jimmy Kapadia suspected, he began selling smuggled goods. While his boys took over the moonshine business, he sold pricey booze, silks, watches, electronic goods. He roped in Imelda to sell stuff for him.

"Not to Dhobi Talao people. They were poor, kadka. I sold maal to people who came to drink. All kinds of people came to my bar, let me tell you. Some of them are page three types. I see them in the papers and I think saala, I know you, you got drunk at my place, caused a scene and nearly got me into trouble."

"Who were his boys?"

"Half-and-halfs like him. You met Homi Sukhadia."

In general, those were good times for Imelda. She was making money, unlike her husband, a drunk, who after being kicked out of too many jobs was unemployable. He played cards with pals, drank, lay about the house in an alcoholic coma. Imelda encouraged his drinking, supplying him with the cheap, lethal stuff she sold. He had, early on in their marriage, wrecked her fantasy of a happy life together. Stanley Braganza was a gentleman till they walked down the aisle. Immediately afterwards he revealed himself to be capricious, prone to violent tempers. He would beat her till she could barely walk. Twice she miscarried because Stanley slammed her against the wall because dinner wasn't ready on time or he thought he saw her exchanging meaningful glances with one of his friends in church. The beatings slowed down once Stanley began seriously drinking. Since he couldn't hold a job for long, Imelda began to work to feed the three of them.

"Daru, not Jesus Christ, was my saviour," Imelda said.

So she allowed him as much booze as he wanted since it kept him sedated and hastened his death. When Stanley did die, prematurely as Imelda had wanted, it wasn't from a rotten liver, though alcohol was involved. Stanley, who didn't have a noble tissue in his wasted body, decided one night to intervene in a drunken brawl in the neighbourhood. In his attempt to shield the weaker party, he was hit hard on the head by a flailing arm holding an empty bottle of hooch. He staggered to the ground, giving the fellow he was trying to save a chance to escape. Three days later, he was dead from cerebral edema. Instead of feeling joy, Imelda was wracked with guilt. The one time Stanley tried to help someone resulted in his death by a bottle that she had, in all likelihood, provided.

"I thought the day that bugger dies, I'll throw a party. I'll send mutton chops and bibinca to all the neighbours. I thought I had the heart of a man. But we are women, we're always guilty. We can be haramis but we can't sleep peacefully afterwards like a man."

Then came the loneliness. Even a stupefied Stanley was better than having no one around. At least he was a presence, a sign of life despite the miasma of booze and perspiration he radiated. After Philomena left for Canada, Imelda quit selling daru and smuggled stuff and got a job as a night-time ayah for elderly women. To make a little more cash, she began a small catering business in the day.

"Jesus told me I had to serve people if I wanted peace of mind. You saw me with Mrs Peters. Do you think I have peace of mind? But I had to do what the Lord ordered or I would not be able to sleep."

—

Before leaving the city, Burjor had stayed with Imelda for a couple of days. He was in hiding and the strategic layout of Imelda's house meant he would be alerted in time to escape if anyone came for him. He told her about leaving me with Mini and asked if she could somehow keep an eye, make sure I was being looked after. And so, pretending to be an itinerant seller of cakes and biscuits, Imelda began to ring our Colaba doorbell every fortnight.

"Two-three days before, I would bake some tutti-frutti sponge cake and butter biscuits, enough to fill a small bag. It was good dhanda. Many people in your building bought from me."

But never Ratna, who would answer the door, often with me in her arms. Ratna, with her natural suspicion of and dislike for most people, would rudely shoo Imelda away. Imelda, penitent after the death of her husband, couldn't help seeing every request for help as a divine imperative. She swallowed her impulse to shout right back at Ratna and returned every fortnight for several months. Only once she'd gathered enough intelligence from the building watchman, who she'd befriended, and glimpsed enough snatches of me contentedly sitting in Ratna's arms before the door was slammed in her face, did she feel satisfied that I was in good hands. Later, I confirmed her story with Ratna, who did indeed remember being annoyed every fortnight by a cake-selling lady.

"Aami oke protyek baar boltam, please tomhara baje cake leke chaala jao." I would tell her every time, take your shitty cake and leave.

"Na kheye ki kore bolle cake ta baje?" How could you say the cake was bad without eating it?

"Mohila ta Christian. Ora shuor aar beeph khaye. Oder hather ranna aami kono din khabona." The woman was Christian. They cook pork and beef. There's no way I'm eating food made by their hands.

"Ami-o beef khai." I eat beef too.

"Maya, ei bapar-e thathha korishne." Don't joke about this issue.

The one aspect of Burjor's story that I was ignorant about was why he had to leave Bombay. People like to tell stories from the start, from event to event in temporal progression, without interruption. Homi, Hilla and Jimmy were committed to drawing a detailed portrait of Burjor before giving up the punchline.

"Oh, you don't know?" Imelda said. "He killed a man."

21

Philomena's story had a strangely unsettling effect on Mini. In fact, she'd get agitated every time I brought up Burjor's liaisons. It was as if she was hearing about the transgressions of a boyfriend. The depth of feeling she had for him seemed disproportionate to their brief flirtation. It occurred to me that perhaps Mini's possessiveness was fanned by the fact that she was the mother of Burjor's child, a connection that was intimate despite the distance of years. Needing a target, she directed some of her anger towards me. I was just like him in my attitude to the opposite sex, incapable of real feeling, tossing away relationships as casually as throwing away old clothes. Logic flew out of the window when Mini, normally a rational person, got angry. Her voice acquired a tremolo and her naturally sharp tongue grew sharper.

"I don't know why you had to inherit this quality. You could have inherited some of his spirit. He was a go-getter, unlike you," Mini said.

"Let's get one thing straight. Romantic tendencies are *not* congenital."

"He thought he could have fun and get away with it. But there's always a price. In his case, he paid the price with you. Don't think you're going to get away scot-free."

"Why is it so hard for you to accept that none of my boyfriends were right for me? Why are you in a hurry to see me married?"

"If none of them were right, why did you go out with them for months and years? Was it for the sex? How much do you want? To think that you've slept with so many men!"

"You're a pretend feminist. Actually, you're a bigot."

"And you don't understand a thing. You may not be but I'm concerned about your health."

"Don't give me that bullshit. I take precautions. You just find the idea of women sleeping with multiple men distasteful. You just stopped short of calling me a slut."

"Don't be crass, Maya. I want you to get settled because that's what parents want for their children. People get married, have kids. It's nothing to scoff at."

"We all know how well that worked out for you."

"You think your situation is something to envy? Thirty-four, single, living at home. When men grow older, they become more powerful. The money makes them attractive to younger women and some men even manage to hold on to their looks. Look at Burjor, he was years older than the women he courted. But as women grow older, they lose their looks, they become unattractive to men their age or older because those guys are chasing young girls."

"Well done! That's genius insight."

"It's true and you know it. The only thing good about your situation is that you don't have to pay rent."

"So now it's about money? Should I increase my monthly contribution to the household kitty, should I live here like a paying guest? No, better yet, I should move out. Then I'll be out of your hair and I'll have a place to take boys home at night. Plus, you and Shivaji, who never wanted me anyway, can have more freedom to play out your newfound romance."

"Don't disrespect your father. He took you in, gave you a good life, when Burjor abandoned you. Be grateful."

"The truth at last!" I said, feeling the burn of tears. "If I was your flesh and blood, I could've said that rearing kids is a one-way street. Since you have them for selfish reasons, you can't attach conditions. But I'm not. If you hadn't taken me in, things could've been a lot worse for me. For that, you want me to grovel."

"Oh, stop feeling sorry for yourself!"

Usually after big fights, which were rare between Mini and me, we didn't speak for some days. Then Mini would make the first overture and we'd call a truce. This time, after three days of no communication, Mini suggested we smoke a doobie after dinner. It was painful to look into her eyes. They were full of guilt—

she knew she'd crossed a line—and hope that we would reconcile like we'd always done. But I turned her down by wordlessly going to my room, loath to let her off so easily. Adept in the skill of manipulating parents, like most kids, I knew Mini wouldn't last more than a day of silence. I was the best thing that had happened to her. In an apocalyptic scenario in which she had to choose between Shivaji and me—one of us would survive, the other would be sacrificed to the deity of an orthodox, tribal regime—she would hand Shivaji over without a thought. Sure enough, a day later, as I was serenely reading the papers, she threw her arms around me and sobbed into my shoulder. "Maya, I'm sorry, I'm sorry! Talk to me please. I love you."

Mini's outburst made me think once again about my attitude to men. As an exercise in self-reflection, I sat on the chair in my room one night—not the bed since it was too comfortable, hence unsuitable for rigorous thought—and contemplated the history of my relationships. Before Kersi, there was Karan, the photographer. A lovely fellow but easily seduced by shamanic practices such as reiki and crystal healing. The only worthwhile practice he followed was yoga, the vigorous ashtanga variety. He was terrifically fit and his libido had only waxed at an age at which men slowed down sexually and women, on the crest of a hormonal wave, can think of nothing but sex. There was Imran. He had model-like looks and a body like a mannequin. But he was vain and disapproved of my sloppy dressing, my lack of exercise.

The relationships had all been relatively short-lived, rarely exceeding a year. I'd enjoyed them but the only time I felt truly engaged was in bed. Out of the bedroom, I couldn't summon a feeling deeper than fondness for any of them. The idea of marriage was farfetched, even though all, despite their eccentricities, were terrific candidates. Even Kersi, if you were willing to settle for mundane conversation. After all, didn't they say it was too much to expect a man to be everything at once? What a conceit to want someone who was kind, generous, funny, capable of making conversation, intelligent, wise, a money maker! Yet, they could all imagine a future with me and struggled to cross the moat I'd dug restricting real intimacy. They were disappointed that I gave them "too much space", texted and called infrequently, preferred to spend weekends reading rather than hanging out, wasn't hung up on monogamy.

Was I imitating Burjor, who surrounded himself with an aura women found impossible to breach? Was he simply the average libidinous commitment-phobe? Or did he keep himself at arm's length to avoid being buffeted the way he'd been in early life? Two figures came to mind: Nietzsche and one of the gurus Shivaji went to during his spiritual phase. Both were of the belief that our natures are moulded by history as well as inherited traits. (That's as far as the coincidence went.) Nietzsche suggested that we have a *fatum*, a solid kernel implacable in the face of life's forces. No matter what, some things about one don't change. Was the Burjor-like distance I kept from men, a pithy quality sustained by a fearful nature, my inherited *fatum*?

There was nothing really the men had in common to suggest I was subconsciously searching for a type. What did they see in me? Mini was mystified at the amount of male attention I got but this was partly out of jealousy for she'd been with one person her entire life and shrunk from going any further with Burjor.

"I see the immediate appeal," Mini said. "You're attractive, though not remarkable. Skinny. I suppose some men like that. Personally, I prefer curves. But that's not your fault. You're smart, opinionated, you can talk knowledgeably about politics, books, Bombay history. But you're willingly stuck in this dead-end job that's dulling your brain. Have you thought of a career path? No. You have a laissez-faire attitude to everything. If I don't push you to clean your room or exercise, you won't do it. It took you years to look into Burjor's life and only because I was on your case. Your reflexes have slowed, you talk slowly."

"Stop exaggerating!"

Sitting in my less than comfortable chair, I wondered what I was looking for in a man. I'd recently had a disturbing sex dream involving Karela. He was younger, his face was indistinct but I knew it was him. It had occurred in the shallow stupor between sleep and wakefulness, a moment when dreams forcefully grip the dreamer. When I had nightmares in this state, I could sense myself crying out and struggling against an assailant. Sex dreams that took place in this trance, on the other hand, ended in powerful orgasms that shook me awake. After my morning spasm, I woke up and picturing Karela as he actually was, ageing, grizzled, felt repulsed. From what I recalled of the dream, I'd been excited more by Karela's commanding tone than his blurry physicality. He'd made various sexual demands, which I'd performed, and I was excited to have been dominated. Did I want to be instructed? Was the dream an indication of a desire for authority, an Oedipal craving for a father-like figure? Deprived of an assertive male figure growing up—Shivaji only asserted himself to compare me to my over-achieving Calcutta cousins—was I looking for one in a partner? Like Mini, Karela was encouraging yet brutally frank. And enlightened in a world-weary way. When I met him so many years after school, I'd had the fleeting thought that he was the sort of father I would've liked. At the end of my seated meditation, I crawled into my pillowy burrow slightly sickened by the thought that perhaps what I wanted was a bossy partner.

22

Once Homi returned, we continued my education in Burjor studies. He'd spent a week travelling through villages in Gujarat, where Parsis continue to live, with an NGO. Impoverished descendants of Parsi men and tribal women, they were handed out food, clothes, money. This is what he'd meant by taking off to see "my people". It was continuation of a practice he'd begun in the seventies when he was in Burjor's employ.

We were walking towards the Gateway of India, taking the circuitous path through the streets of Fort, past the stock exchange, through the Horniman Circle garden, in and out of the lanes of Kala Ghoda. The plan was to walk down the seafront at Apollo Bunder, cross Arthur Bunder Road, turn right at Colaba Causeway and wrap up with a greasy brunch at Olympia. I had my tour guide routine planned—I would deliver brief biographics of the Horniman Circle area, the institutions in Kala Ghoda, the unremarkable looking yet historically rich buildings on the road to the Gateway, the Gateway itself, the handsome, bigbalconied buildings overlooking the sea and the vast edifices on Arthur Bunder Road that were built to store cotton, then became an arcade of brothels and now had art galleries and boutiques. But I didn't say a word because Homi was once again disclosing astonishing events with no prefatory warning in his flat narrative style.

Homi and Burjor met at a hole-in-the-wall joint in Mazagaon where dockworkers used to go for cheap meals. Homi was a dockhand and at the time Burjor had just started a smuggling racket that would remain minor but make him and his colleagues a decent amount of money.

"What does a decent amount of money mean?" I asked Homi.

Homi couldn't say but he'd seen Burjor stow bundles of cash in the safe at home. And he had himself made a tidy sum that he'd invested in stock.

"What did he do with it? You can't put so much cash in the bank."

"Obviously not. When he'd collected enough, the idea was to put it in real estate. Boss always had a plan, saw ten steps ahead. Bombay was not this kachra-peti of buildings then. Land was being reclaimed, new new buildings were coming up everywhere. He wanted to get into construction. If he didn't have to run with all his money, you might have been a rich young lady."

"About his having to run away. I know he killed a man. Imelda told me. Why don't you start from there and then work backwards? Please Homi uncle, no more suspense."

"Moonie, I will tell you one by one, in sequence. No aage-peechhe."

Burjor recruited Homi, who was desperately poor and unscrupulous. It was his job to oversee the landing of imported goods that had been sent by Madhu Pereira from East Africa and Dubai. Pereira, who had introduced Burjor to the liquor business, had moved to Dubai in the sixties. He went to and fro between Dubai and Kenya, sourcing textiles, watches, electronic goods, booze, which were packed off to Bombay's coast by sea. Burjor and Homi bribed the customs officials to let them take the goods away without paying duty. Their operation was a modest one, small in scale compared to the big-league guys. For instance, they would never have made it to the cinematic event that took place in April of 1977, when around eighty smugglers pledged to end their dealings in contraband in a hospital auditorium before Jayaprakash Narayan, who gave a rousing speech.

"It was just drama. After Emergency, everyone was back in action," said Homi.

Burjor and Homi never dealt in the most lucrative commodity, gold. Business took a hit just before the Emergency, when the Bombay police cracked down on smugglers. Homi spent time in police custody once on the whim of a customs official who Burjor had ticked off by bargaining over the bribe. It was the first of two occasions Homi would go to jail because of Burjor.

Burjor would store some of the stuff in his house in Naval Baug, some in the boot of his Ambassador taxi and, later, in the rented section of a warehouse. He'd drive to the homes of his clients to show and sell his goods. Only the regulars would occasionally be allowed to come over to Naval Baug. Burjor had to keep things quiet; some of neighbours, the fellows he'd scrapped with in the past, would make trouble if they found out. He acquired buyers by discretely spreading a word at aunty bars, where well-off folks came to drink. Or he'd eavesdrop on conversations that took place in the backseat of his cab and gauge his patrons before saying he could get them a good toaster, a fancy watch, a bottle of Johnnie Walker.

At the time, Homi shared a room with five men, all labourers like him, in a chawl in Mazagaon. He thought that that was his life; he would live in the company of single men in a mephitic room, labour for the next thirty years and when his body became arthritic from the heaving and lifting, he would drink himself to an early death. Having a family was out of the question; there was no way he could afford even to marry. And who would find him a wife? There was no family back home, no relatives looking out for him. It was only when the money began coming in that Homi started to dream of a different life.

"Burjor could be a rascal. I told him, don't do mara-mari over the bribe. But he thought he could get away with anything. That one week I spent in custody for him was the worst of my life. Solid beating I got. See my nose." Clearly damaged, it listed to one side like an unfastened sail. "Don't misunderstand, I'm grateful to boss also."

"Did you marry?"

"Moonie, what I told you? One by one."

"So there was someone."

"There was a girl I liked, Meher. Actually, I was in love with her, and for some time, I think she loved me. But then she moved on."

"Moved on how?"

The only connections Homi had with his hometown were a few boys from his orphanage. They were all fifty-fifties like him. One of them, Jal, wrote to Homi saying he wanted to move to Bombay. Was there any way Homi could get him a job? He knew some bookkeeping; he could work in a shop or the accounts department of a company. The only person with any connections Homi knew was Burjor. Keen to help a fellow fifty-fifty, Burjor got Jal a job with one of his businessmen clients. Jal, whose father had spawned a large brood of halfling kids with several women, had a half-brother who wanted to come to Bombay. Burjor got him a job in a mill with the help of a neighbour in Naval Baug, a prominent member of the factory's trade union. He got another boy from the orphanage a job as a salesman at Pesi Desai's spectacles shop. This was after his affair with Pesi's wife, Hufrish, beautiful, generously proportioned and frustrated by her husband's erectile defect, and before she and her husband migrated to Canada. What a terrific guy! To help a fellow Parsi out at the request of your romantic rival.

It was then that Burjor performed his real pirate act, a daring combination of commerce and philanthropy. After getting Jal and the other two jobs in the city, Burjor sensed an opportunity. The villages in Gujarat were full of fifty-fifties living in poverty. The ones that made their way to Bombay usually ended up as cleaners in fire temples or low-level workers within the Parsi administrative universe. Why not start an employment agency just for them? Jobs in exchange for a percentage of salary. Homi, who was made a partner, made trips to Vansda, Anklesar, Bharuch, Navsari to spread the word. That was one thing Burjor wouldn't do, revisit the state of his birth.

"So he ran the liquor business, smuggled stuff and managed the employment agency?" I said.

"Yes. I was his right-hand man, mind you."

"Where were you guys going with this? The agency would've made you peanuts."

"I told you, construction."

Burjor's grand agenda was to get into the construction business, which at the time was thriving in Bombay. Buildings were coming up on reclaimed land, neighbourhoods that are now exploding were scrub and marsh. Mini always complained that Shivaji could've bought a place in Cuffe Parade, which was being built on reclaimed earth. If he had listened to her, they could've been living in an apartment worth tens of crores. But his parents, those fools, thinking that such a building would have shaky foundations and eventually collapse into the sea, convinced their son not to buy. The best part of Burjor's plan was that the company would be staffed mostly by fifty-fifties.

"He thought of reservation before anyone else," Homi crowed.

"To be sure, many family-run companies hire people from their own communities," I said. Making pragmatic interjections in stories was a bad habit of mine. Homi ignored me.

"We could have become Raheja, Shapoorji Pallonji. Can you imagine?"

23

Could I imagine? I was lightheaded from what I was hearing. The employment agency was an ingenious idea. A malt-coloured cab driver-turned-hooch-dealer-turned-smuggler elevating his fellow half-and-halfs under the noses of zealots was an inspiring tale. The scale of the operation was small but what ambition, what cheek! Had he not had to flee the city, I don't doubt Burjor would've risen to the top of the construction industry, lifting up with his giant palm his country cousins.

Could he have made it to the league of great Zoroastrians? The company of businessmen-philanthropists, extraordinary hustlers who began with nothing and ended with giant fortunes, palaces on hilltops, vast seaside mansions, antiquities that now filled galleries in the city museum, silks, grand institutions whose stone buildings had a balm-like effect on my fluttering nerves. Listening to Homi, it seemed possible. Burjor had the right solution of qualities, a mix of ambition, opportunism, imagination, tenacity, generosity and a considerable degree of ruthlessness. It was such a combination that had mobilized the Jeejeebhoys and Tatas of the exemplary Zoroastrian universe. In school, Karela loved to tell us about Jamsetjee Jeejeebhoy, who, orphaned at sixteen, barely tutored, went on to become Bombay's greatest merchant prince.

"He made crores in the nineteenth century," Karela had said. "Do you know how much that would be worth now? I don't. It's beyond my comprehension. All from shovelling opium down Chinese pipes. The man financed half of Bombay's great institutions. But the Chinese paid the price. Essentially he, and all the other big opium fellows, the Tatas, Readymoneys, were smugglers. The trade was illegal. Heard of the opium war? I want you to look it up during your next library period. The Indian merchants pretty much financed the war. You won't find this stuff in the anthologies of great Parsis. Now I know that Scherezade here (pointing to a mousy girl, who we made fun of for wearing her hair in a braid that hung from the side of her head like a hirsute proboscis, and later praised for being ahead of her time when we identified the style as 'ghetto') belongs to a family that was involved in the opium business. Later, they switched to the more respectable industry of textiles, like a lot of merchants. Sherry, I'm sure you have lots of books in your living room of illustrious Parsis. Look them up when you get time from styling your hair. Now why is it that they're touchy about their past? Because it's embarrassing. Opium is not cool in this day and age."

The next day we heard that Karela was hauled up by the principal for disparaging certain families. Obviously Sherry was the rat. Her father was one of the trustees of the school. One of my classmates avenged Karela on behalf of all of us by yanking Sherry's plait with painful force.

These thoughts swam through my mind as Homi ploughed on and I imagined I could see the ferocious spirit of Bombay's great barons driving Burjor. At the same time, I found it distasteful that he took a cut from the pay of people he helped with employment. To take a percentage from the first salary of a labourer or pickle maker...

"We weren't doing charity, Moonie," Homi said. "We had not reached that level."

Since the operation was carried out of Burjor's home in Naval Baug, it had to be secret. The place was full of diehards and rednecks, who, suspecting Burjor's mixed extraction, secretly called him 'dubra', the malicious name applied to tribals. For them it was bad enough that the fifty-fifties were officially Parsi; to give them a real leg-up was anathema.

Naturally, it was all informal. Homi and Burjor took cash and maintained records in a register. The unskilled fellows were sent to work in the mills, docks, construction sites, factories, kitchens. The ones with some skill were set up in accounting and administration departments of companies, in shops. There were women too. They were set up as ayahs, factory workers, nurses, secretaries. If they lacked the money for a nursing or secretarial course, Burjor would pay for it. He offered lines of credit to those wanting to start small businesses. In the brief life of the agency, Burjor and Homi helped nearly seventy men and women.

"Have you heard of Piloo's Pickles? They're famous in Dadar. Piloo came from a village near Navsari with nothing. She was staying in the home of a woman from her village who was a kind person and did a lot of social work. Now Piloo knew how to cook. First, she started cooking in people's homes. Then she heard about Burjor through someone like us working in one of the houses she used to go to. She came to us for a small loan and started making pickles. They sold like hot cakes. Burjor said, 'Pay me the interest in achar.' So every month she would send us prawn, brinjal, carrot and fish pickles."

Not everyone had connections in Bombay. Homi had lived on the street till he could afford a spot in the chawl. As word spread and more fifty-fifties began writing to them seeking jobs, Burjor let a few men stay in a warehouse in Wadi Bunder after securing them work. He'd rented a corner of the warehouse to keep his contraband. The men had three months to find a place to live; not more than ten could stay at a time.

"Then there's a guy called Eruch. We got him a job as a peon in a law firm. I knew he would go up in life. He was willing to do anything. If you told him, 'My wife is having an affair with this guy. Help me bump him off. I'll pay you so much', he would do it. Because he was very poor; he used to go hungry back home. Anyway, so Eruch started as a peon. He used to make chai, take documents from one cabin to another, deliver parcels, be a server in the boss's house when there was a party, etcetera etcetera. From peon he became admin head. Now a peon made him chai. It was a small firm, there weren't too many people between the peon and the boss. But still, it was quite a jump. Then he joined the admin department of a bigger company and retired as vice president of the department! Sala, used to call me Homi sir, Homi sir. I met him once when he was a big man. He shook my hand and said 'Hello Homi, kem chhe?' Now he was the sir."

One of the fellows was a moderately famous actor, whose shtick was playing the bumbling Parsi in movies and TV serials. In his most recent film, which was a hit, Dinyar essayed an affable Parsi with a gummy grin.

"That guy! He looks like he's of pure Iranian descent," I said.

"He's gone on his father obviously."

Burjor got him a job as an electrician at Patkar Hall with the help of Hilla and Jimmy. The two of them spent a lot of time at the theatre as actors in Adi Marzban's troupe. Dinyar was a joker, always horsing around and playing the fool. He caught Marzban's ear. Being from the hinterland, he spoke better Gujarati than the Bombay fellows, who talked with a precious Anglicized lilt, and knew obscure idioms. The director, known for cleverly manipulating Parsi-Gujarati to produce risqué punchlines, cast him in a couple of plays, most notably as an oafish Irani servant. He made a huge impression on the audience, which, one night, included a movie producer. The man gave Dinyar a bit part in a film and that was the start of his career.

"I read about Keki Mehta in the papers," I said. "The man with the masala empire, who died recently. The article mentioned Burjor, that he'd given Mehta a loan to start his business. I nearly had a heart attack when I saw Burjor's name."

"I knew Keki. His nails used to be yellow because whole day he made masala."

Keki used to work as a cook in a wealthy Parsi home. He started out as the cleaner and odd jobs man and he'd occasionally cook meals for the staff. His employers happened to taste his cooking one evening. So impressed were they, Keki was soon elevated to the position of khansama, sous chef.

"He used to make prawn dhansak," Homi said. "Have you ever heard of that here? These Bombay Parsis don't know Parsi food actually. It was out of this world, I tell you."

It was Piloo who led Keki to Burjor. Before her business seriously took off, Piloo would go door to door with her bag of pickles. One of the homes she called at frequently was the one where Keki worked. They became friends, Keki would occasionally invite her in and offer her a cutlet, a bowl of daal and rice, a plate of fish curry. Keki ground all the masalas himself, following recipes he'd learned at home in Gujarat. From Burjor, he procured a line of credit and started his masala business, which, when it grew significant enough to name, he called it Keki's Magic Masalas.

"What about Meher?"

24

Meher was better off than the others. Both her parents were fifty-fifties and her father was a teacher in a school in Valsad. Now Meher had been a good student, she was popular among kids, and adults had marked her as the responsible sort. She was expected to marry after school, keep a good home, make babies, care for her aging parents and so on. (This is the account she gave Homi.) She altered the course of this trajectory ordained by her family and social circle by falling for a neighbour and getting knocked up. For four months, Meher kept quiet, praying for a miscarriage, paralyzed by fear of her parents and neighbours finding out and the shame that would fall on her. Then her stomach began to swell and her shrewd mother knew for certain immediately. She'd already noticed the flush in Meher's complexion and the slight heaviness in her breasts. She slapped her daughter a couple of times, extracted the truth and in a covert operation took her to a quack in Navsari. Valsad was too small a town; everyone was bound to find out. There were murmurs already among the neighbourhood's seasoned women, who were quick to spot the bodily signs. In Navsari, the quack performed a barbaric operation, inserting a metal instrument into Meher to get her to bleed.

"She told you all this personal stuff?" I asked. We were rapidly approaching our final stop, Olympia.

"We lived together like man and wife for eight months."

Meher's folks were terribly unnerved by the episode, especially the father, a man of delicate mind and constitution. Years later, he became an early victim of Alzheimer's. When he lost his mind, he would defecate around the house and, occasionally, on the neighbour's porch. Her mother, sick of tending to him and sweeping his itinerant faecal deposits, blamed Meher for seeding his decline. Their immediate response was to pack her off to Bombay, far from the wagging tongues of the neighbourhood. Here she lived as a paying guest with a family from Valsad her parents knew, and took secretarial classes at Davar's College in Fort. It was there that she befriended Havovi, the shorthand teacher and the first woman Burjor and Homi had helped. Havovi introduced her to Homi.

"She didn't need you to get her a job. She could've got one herself," I said. We were at Olympia, working our way through kheema, bheja and chicken kebabs.

"True. But when you need a job, you try everything."

"How did Havovi know about Meher? It's not like fifty-fifties talk about themselves openly."

"Meher didn't look Parsi at all. She was very dark—one of her grandmothers was Siddi."

I had to stop for a second, shoving a morsel of roti-wrapped goat brain into my right cheek, to contemplate Meher's genetic make-up. Parsi, adivasi and Siddi, blood of a small community that was transported to the country as East African soldiers and slaves, whose members went on to become rulers of minor principalities and now lived in clusters in Gujarat, Maharashtra and a few other spots along the west coast. In Bombay, in Dongri, I had seen Siddi Goma, the ritual dance in which they painted their faces and wore grassy skirts and headgear. It was a strange and wonderful expression of their Bantu roots transposed to a foreign environment, foreign because though they'd lived here for centuries, the Siddis, with their African faces and hair, were relatively little-known. Did Meher have a hard time growing up in a small town with dark skin and pronounced African features? (She'd taken entirely after the Siddi grandmother.) Not really, Homi said, explaining that despite the orthodoxy, there was a degree of tolerance among small town folk for mixed progeny. Of course, that vanished when scale and drama entered the picture, which is what happened at Burjor's navjote in 1942.

Burjor and Homi got Meher a job as a secretary in a small company through the offices of Eruch, the wily peon who had made friends in several firms in the Fort area where he worked. Of course, there was a modest incentive in it for him. Once she began working, she moved into the Parsi working women's hostel in Worli, where she stayed until she was kicked out. Once again, the cause of her trouble was a man. This time, the guy was her boss, who was married and had children. In a classic turn of events, Meher was spotted making out with her boss (Homi delicately said they were "cosy like") outside the gate of the hostel. He would occasionally drop her home, taking care to pull up some distance away. This time, they were seen by a couple of Meher's hostel mates, who were walking home after a stroll on Worli Sea Face. Unfortunately, the witnesses happened to be two aging, impoverished ladies, who'd been abandoned by their families and had for years lived in the hostel. The trust that ran the hostel allowed them to continue even though they had no means to pay the fee. In return for this largesse, the crones spied on the hostel's young girls for the warden, keeping track of when they came in for the night (the daily deadline was eight-thirty), who they were with and so on. Scandals like this lit up their dark lives for days, warmed the blood in their frigid veins. Had Meher been seen with an unmarried man, the warden would've let her off with a withering scolding for being affectionate in public. But when, on questioning Meher's friends (the old ladies were also inquisitors), it was discovered that the man in the car matched the description of her boss and that he was married, the warden told her to leave.

Now Meher had few friends. In fact, she seemed to get along better with men than women. I liked to imagine that Meher, with her chocolatey skin and exotic face was one of those girls who radiate a sexual aura that other women find threatening. Naturally, she turned to her fellow fifty-fifty Homi, who, besotted with her, took her into his one-room home in the Byculla chawl.

"What happened to the boss?" We had taken the impromptu decision to have dessert. Homi was fond of the rum balls at the Ratan Tata Institute down the road. It was there that we walked.

The boss was no help. When Meher turned to him, he said he had a wife and kids to think about. There was no way he could accommodate her. They fought and the man, fearing Meher would reveal herself to his family, threw her out of the job. Going home to Valsad was out of the question. Her parents were still coming to terms with her teenage misdemeanour. If they learned of the latest scandal, who knows, they might be felled by a stroke, suffer a nervous breakdown. In this vulnerable state, she went to Homi.

Was it genuine feeling or a mix of gratitude and desperate cunning that drove Meher to play the part of a wife for eight months? It pained me to think of Homi, puffed with love and hope as he hurried home every evening to dinner made by Meher's dear hands. To be the protector of this ingénue irresistible to predatory men...he had something to look forward to for the first time in his life. The neighbours were told they'd had a secret wedding as her parents were opposed to the match. The chawl folks were excited by the drama, having no trouble buying Homi's story as this was a common occurrence. And Homi wasn't seriously concerned when Meher responded to his proposal of marriage by saying they ought to wait even though she was eager in her affection.

"Burjor warned me you know," Homi said. "He told me something is not right." We were sitting at a table in RTI under the harsh glare of tubelights, sawing dense rum balls with brittle plastic spoons.

Eight months later, the idyll was over. Meher announced she was getting back with her ex-boss. He would set her up in a small flat, she could have her job back and he promised to work towards asking his wife for a divorce. It turned out they had been in touch not long after Meher had moved to Byculla. How did the boss find out? Inquiries had led to Eruch, the ambitious peon working his way up the administrative ranks in the Fort area. Eruch had provided Homi's address, to which the boss had sent a courier bearing his missive. A series of clandestine meetings took place while Homi was away at work. And one evening, as he returned from a day of cutting dirty deals at the docks, feeling on top of the world, he found Meher standing grimly by her packed bag.

"Burjor said, 'She's even dumber than you to believe that harami boss. He'll never leave his wife.' He was right. She waited for him for some years, then married some much older man. It didn't go well. She wrote to me, you know, one long Ramayan about all her problems.

Her husband wasn't caring enough, they couldn't afford to have a baby, her father had become a mental case and what not. Burjor was no longer here then. He would have told me, 'Homi, don't reply. She wants something from you. Don't fall into that trap again'."

But sweet, guileless Homi couldn't help himself. He responded to her unspoken plea with the alacrity of a lifeguard spotting flailing arms in the water. They met at Regal Restaurant, next to Palace Talkies in Byculla, not far from where Homi lived, and had a long chat that left him feeling hopeful. As they drank milky chai, he began to believe that she'd seen the error of her judgement, that she'd realized that she should've stuck with him. The treachery of hope! At the end of their meeting, he gave her a wad of cash. Meher touched his arm before leaving, which he interpreted as a further sign of her change of heart. Homi never heard from her again; his letters to her went unanswered.

"Burjor would have said, 'She made a chootiya out of you twice and now you're upset. You asked for it'. He would have been right," Homi said, swallowing the maraschino cherry garnishing the rum ball that he'd saved for last.

25

From having a shadow father in Shivaji, I had now acquired three semi-paternal figures, who had begun to make claims on my time. Altaf Arsiwala, Homi's former landlord, rang from his hall of mirrors. I told him about finding Homi in the chaos of the attack's aftermath and that he lived in a fragile building in Fort. A room with a kitchen in his Byculla chawl had just been vacated. Would Homi be interested? The place had an attached bathroom too. The days of using a stinking common toilet were over. "I'll ask him myself," Arsiwala said, excited at the prospect of renewing an acquaintance.

I told Karela about Burjor's employment agency for fifty-fifties. The story electrified him and he ordered me to write a chapter on it in his book, the rogue's gallery of Parsis. He'd found someone willing to put up the money to publish the book, a young poker buddy.

"Like a lot of Parsi kids, he inherited a considerable amount of money from a couple of childless relatives. So he doesn't need to work. He spends his time playing poker and managing his wealth. And because he has the grace to feel guilty over his privilege, he spends some of his cash on altruistic things. You'll be happy to know he's investing in an upcoming news website committed to honest reportage. Unlike your garbage paper."

For the chapter in Karela's book, I met Piloo the pickle lady. Piloo invited me to her workshop in an industrial estate in Andheri. From this aromatic room, hundreds of bottles of pickles—lemon, mango, chilli, garlic, mixed veg, prawn, fish roe, brinjal—were dispatched across the country. As soon as you entered, the sharp odours of chilli and mustard darted up the nose. Piloo led me to her office eyrie from where she surveyed her workers, all women, fermenting and bottling the pungent stuff.

"First you try," she said, pointing to a row of bowls filled with pickles and a stack of thepla.

"Piloo aunty, I can't handle spice," I said, patting my belly to indicate a weak stomach.

"It's spicy but not hot. Nothing will happen."

She was wrong. Every bite, from the whole clove of garlic and wedge of lemon to the chunk of roe and chilli she insisted was on the weak end of the scale, released a cloud of heat in my body. At the end of the tasting, I was red and gasping. I truly felt the consequences, as I knew I would, in a blazing torrent in the toilet later in the day.

"Now ask what you want to ask," she said.

Both Piloo's parents were fifty-fifties in a village

near Navsari. They were dirt poor and they died young, leaving their daughter with nothing. By then, Piloo was working as a cook in a Parsi home.

"Basically, I had no fall-back option," she said.

But working for others was not a long-term option either. Piloo was a forceful personality, she liked giving orders, not taking them. Short and squat, a female Joe Pesci, she sat with both arms splayed across her desk, a stance that suggested an aggressive force, and covered herself in signs of power. She wore a thick gold watch, gold rings and a chain with a chunky asho farohar pendant. Her tone, when she commanded me to sample her pickles, was peremptory. Through the fifty-fifty grapevine, she came across Burjor, who loaned her the capital to start the business. At the time, she was living in the staff quarters of a bungalow in Tardeo. It was here that she began her operation.

"Homi said you paid Burjor back in pickle?" I said.

"What nonsense! Pickle was extra. I paid him back his capital plus one and a half per cent interest mind you."

"Did you have trouble paying him back?"

"Once I had to ask Burjor for an extension. But I couldn't keep doing that. He was a hardcore guy, you understand."

"Did that bother you? You were poor. He could've been more lenient."

"Ya, it was tough. Back then I thought he was a bit of a rascal. But I don't know, maybe I would have done the same. You know who helped me when I found it difficult to pay back? Your mummy, Armaity."

Armaity was Piloo's pickle taster. She was a terrific cook herself and had a keen palate that could, Piloo said, divine the flavour of each ingredient in an item. Piloo would calibrate her formulas according to Armaity's exact appraisal. And when Piloo struggled to pay Burjor an instalment, Armaity would loan her the cash.

"So you paid Burjor with his own money?" I said.

"Ya. And I paid Armaity back over time."

"Did she help others this way?"

"I don't think so. But she helped us in other ways. Whenever you went to their house, Armaity would serve you a hot meal. She gave us biscuits to take home or some snack she had made. For some of us, there was no guarantee we would get three meals a day."

Hot tears that had nothing to do with the pickle burned my eyes and I had to blink rapidly while burying my head in my notebook. If Piloo thought my sudden folding motion odd, if she spotted the warm drop on the page, she said nothing. Armaity, who, eclipsed by Burjor, occupied only a small part of my imagination, now loomed larger than a footnote in Burjor's enterprise. The reluctant husband had kept her out of his life, his grand project. But she had quietly made her own contribution. I felt a swell of emotion—was it sadness or the strange sensation of feeling affection for someone you never knew?—for this kind woman, whose youthful joie de vivre was crushed by marriage to Burjor. What remarkable actions, big or small, would she have performed had she lived? Where would I have been with Armaity around? How would my mind have developed in the universe of Naval Baug?

Piloo packed me off with pickles she had recently introduced to the market, with deadly condiments including, chillies from the North-East. I gave these to Hilla and Jimmy Kapadia, when I paid them an overdue visit. I wanted to corroborate Homi's story. What did they know? Did they wonder about the people visiting Burjor? What was the word in the colony? The place was like a village; everyone knew what the other person was up to. But they'd had only a sketchy idea till the drama that revealed their friend's activities. How did a story like this escape the press? It would've been explosive. I could see the headlines. 'The Bogey of Mixed Blood "Parsis" Rears Its Head Again' (in a conservative Zoroastrian paper), 'Baug Bounty: Meet The Good Samaritan Who Helps Poor Mixed Parsis Get Jobs' (in the average English daily), 'Saviour or Sinner? The Man Who Helps Mixed Parsis Get Work' (in a tabloid).

"According to Homi, Burjor got a lot of visitors in the six months they ran the agency. What did you think was going on?" I said.

"We just assumed they were involved in whatever shady business Burjor was running," Hilla said.

"But these were ordinary folk. Pickle-makers, peons."

"Burjor's life wasn't an open book, you know," Jimmy

said. "We knew there were limits with the guy. You couldn't ask him anything and expect him to answer."

When the truth emerged, it was a scandal. Naval Baug had, in fact, been reeling from a series of major and minor ignominies involving both the residents of the colony and Parsis at large. Not long back, one of the colony boys, a quiet fellow who generally went unnoticed, was jailed. Turned out he was a deadly assassin attached to a rising gang of hot-blooded thugs that was, at the time, eliminating adversaries while staking claim to a piece of the smuggling business. Before him was a national scandal that embarrassed Parsis all over. I got a real kick out of this one, having heard about it from Karela, who told the story with great relish. In 1971, Rustam Nagarwala, an ex-military intelligence guy, apparently impersonated Indira Gandhi on the phone with Ved Malhotra, the head cashier of State Bank of India's Parliament Street branch in Delhi. He said he needed sixty lakhs in cash for a secret operation involving Bangladesh. Apparently—there are few certainties in this case—Malhotra was told that he was to hand over the cash to a courier.

The voice on the phone instructed him to later collect a receipt from the prime minister's residence. When he went over, he was told no such request had been made. The cops were pressed into action. What an embarrassment! What a wild chain of events! Nagarwala was caught that night itself with the cash. He was swiftly tried and sentenced to four years without any corroborative evidence. In jail, he declared that there was a real story behind this incredible comedy and there was speculation that Nagarwala was indeed on a mission to swiftly procure cash for the Bangladesh war by avoiding bureaucratic delay. But he died in the hospital on, according to reports, his fifty-first birthday.

"Malhotra's cue was the code 'Bangladesh ka babu.' Can you believe that?" Karela said, slapping a grizzled thigh that emerged from obscenely short shorts. A couple of paragraphs in the preface of Karela's book were dedicated to the episode.

"The whole thing stinks," I told Karela. "Imitating Indira Gandhi's voice to get cash out? That's right out of a third-rate Hindi movie. I hope you're taking a critical view in the book."

"Of course not. I'm thinking of inserting a cartoon about it."

—

The discovery of Burjor's employment agency occurred in this fraught environment, when the Parsis of Naval Baug were wondering whether the general impression of the Zoroastrian as an honest individual with ironclad integrity was a myth. Could it be that they weren't as pure as the snow on the volcanic slopes of Mount Damavand but as good or morally reprehensible as anyone else? Now unlike the other two, Burjor had done nothing wrong. But the conservatives in the colony were outraged. A mixed Parsi helping people like him to come up in life right under their Persian noses...blasphemous!

"We didn't ask too many questions but others were more curious and made it their business to find out, as you now know," Jimmy said.

26

Homi was in touch with some of the fifty-fifties he and Burjor had helped find employment. They called themselves The Adhkachru Club, the half-cooked society. Eruch, the ambitious peon, was part of the group, so was Piloo. They met once in a while to catch up over chai or for a boozy night out at one of their homes. Some of the Adhkachrus had founded an NGO, whose members had Parsis of all compositions, called Zoroastrians Against Poverty, ZAP. The Zapsters, as they called themselves, travelled to the interiors of Gujarat distributing food, clothes and various useful items to Parsis still living in rustic poverty. Many of the families were descendants of fifty-fifties. They raised money to send kids to college, repair broken roofs, get the sick treated and, in the spirit of Burjor's employment agency, helped young men and women find work. I tagged along with Homi and a small crew of Zapsters on one trip.

The plan was to visit several families living around Ankleshwar. Six of us took the Gujarat Express from Bombay Central at dawn. As we pulled out of the station and sped towards Ankleshwar, I had the unsettling feeling in the pit of my stomach that change was imminent, that I was an arrow waiting, like that grumpy poet and his newly-wed companions, to be released. (It was an inconvenient sensation to be having in a train, where the toilets were terrible, for any emotional churn in that region had the effect of unlocking my intestinal sluices.)

Further north, Shivaji and Mini were on a transformative journey of their own, to Manali. A curious change had begun to take effect after 26/11. Mini and Shivaji had for years settled into a resigned equilibrium. They were like flat mates, who led separate lives. After Shivaji's brush with death, they began showing, with increasing frequency, signs of affection. This was strange for me, who had never seen them hold hands or hug. Kissing was farfetched, practically inconceivable. To see them sitting close to each other on the couch while watching TV, their sides touching, occasionally holding hands, was almost indecent. I had to look away. He was warmer towards me too. Sometimes he'd give me a tentative smile. Once he reached out awkwardly to give me a hug. Alarmed, I turned my body in such a way that his action ended in a pat on the back. Ratna too was bewildered by the sudden revision in her boss and ally. She made efforts to win Shivaji back by cooking elaborate items she'd learned about on Bengali cooking shows on television. Gourds stuffed with cashew and curried, hilsa with pineapple, pea-filled puris to be had with a rich daal, a pulao with mutton ribs. Instead of approbation, Shivaji took up Mini's long-standing grouse with Ratna and told her to cook simpler stuff with less oil.

"The two of you have been like siblings all these years. Now you can't get your hands off each other," I said to Mini one morning, after Shivaji had left for work.

The twelve hours Shivaji had spent trapped in the Taj had turned him completely, Mini said. While waiting to be discovered and shot or led to freedom, Shivaji had experienced a moment of clarity, the kind that great upheavals sometimes deliver. In the brief flash of that inexplicably reflexive moment, his actions from the time he married Mini were laid bare and he realized he'd been an unbearable husband.

"He cried and apologized for being a 'selfish bastard'. That's two firsts—I've never seen him cry before or heard him apologize."

"And that brought your romance back from the dead?"

"Something like that. He also said he thinks your lack of ambition has to do with the fact that he didn't give you enough attention. That you're not where you could be because you lacked at least one pushy parent."

"The other guy is culpable for that. Tell Shivaji he can spare himself the guilt."

"He thinks you should find yourself a guy, get settled. He wants to help."

"How, exactly?"

"By listing your details on a matrimonial website."

"I think I prefer the old Shivaji."

Emboldened by Mini's encouraging response to his mea culpa, Shivaji suggested a holiday. This was astonishing as Shivaji hated leaving the city unless it was to visit his folks in Calcutta. Holidays meant breaking routine, eating unfamiliar food, wearing the same pajamas for a couple of nights to avoid expensive laundry, being dragged by Mini to this monument or that museum. Mini, who liked to see new places, had a group of friends, mostly single or divorced, with whom she travelled every summer. I had accompanied them on a few occasions. Every night, over endless drinks—and joints it was my job to roll when I was old enough—I was privy to intoxicated ribaldry and bitter stories of miserable marriages. At the end of the night, one of them would drunkenly instruct Mini, "For fuck's sake yaar, don't let Maya ruin her life by getting married."

The choice of Manali indicated just how radical this transformation was. If there was anything Shivaji hated more than travelling, it was the cold.

"You're going to the land of monkey-capped Bong tourists with a Bong who will don his monkey cap at the slightest breeze," I said.

"Don't be a snob," she said.

"You're not going to smoke any Malana cream with that prude in tow."

"I'm more interested in seeing things."

"He's only going to want to eat at the Bong joints."

"We'll compromise. Some days we'll eat machher jhol, some days we'll eat at German Bakery."

When the time for them to leave came, Ratna was distraught. She had poured her feelings into the meal she packed for them and hoped that when Shivaji, aboard the train, ate her loochi, aloo bhaja and kosha mangsho, he would be reminded of her faithfulness and sleight of hand in the kitchen, things he'd forgotten in his haste to make amends with her nemesis, Mini. The idea of being home alone, with no one to cook for but herself, for the first time, filled her with profound dread. So formidable was the feeling that Ratna had broken character, clasping Mini before she left and sobbing theatrically into her shoulder, apologizing for behaving badly. She did the same when I left, leaving a damp patch on my t-shirt. As their train sped onwards to Pathankot, from where they would drive to Manali, Ratna felt her hold on Shivaji slipping.

—

Meanwhile, the Adhkachrus and I rushed past fields of green that stood out with startling clarity against the purple, rain-ready clouds. The train clattered evenly at full speed, blasting its tapering honk as it ran past minor stations; dozing bodies rocked in their berths. The Zapsters, familiar with the scenery having made this trip several times, chatted or slept. I kept my eyes on the monsoon verdure.

We raced past Bhilad, Vapi, Udvada, Valsad, Bilimora, Navsari and Surat. Five and a half hours later, we pulled into Ankleshwar, where we camped for the night at a lodge owned by Percy, a ZAP member and our local coordinator. A stocky, sturdy fellow in a safari suit and maroon felt cap, Percy talked a lot very fast, took rapid steps and made swift gestures. He moved so quickly that a few years after driving an auto for a living as a young man, he became the owner of a fleet of autos, followed by a fleet of tempos. He became a local councillor, acquired the lodge and a couple of flats that he rented out.

That evening, we banqueted on the kind of rich, offal-heavy meal that has long gone out of fashion in cities. There was Old Monk and shandy and with drinks, Percy's khansama served fried Bombay Duck, fried chicken liver and mince kebabs. For dinner, he brought out whole goat's head cooked in chana daal; khurchan, a stir-fry of goat kidney, lung and liver; a couple of large pomfrets stuffed with prawn; a tub of creamy rava and jalebis. Percy got drunk and sang dirty Gujarati songs. Everyone agreed they'd need Isabgol, the laxative and essential travel companion, to expel all the animal waste the next morning.

Over two days, Percy's chauffeur drove us to villages where Parsis still lived. Tailing us was a truck bearing food and supplies. The places—Vankal, Zankhvav, Ilav, Boria, Varethpethia...—were far from highways, reached by dirt roads that seemed to be going nowhere. And then suddenly before us, a shabby, low-roofed brick and timber abode. Like the home of Banoo and Dhanji Patel, who lived in Lavet with their teenaged son Jimmy and got by, by selling milk from their cows. Dark-skinned, closer in resemblance to their Hindu neighbours, no one looking at them would say they were Parsi. As the Zapsters doled out rice, daal, grains, a cycle for Jimmy, I picked my way through the homely detritus—a bullock cart wheel, wooden beams, discarded tools, a couple beds and plastic chairs and a table with photos of the dead. Behind the house was a shed where cows fed at a trench.

In another village, Pervin Anklesaria emerged from her hovel in a ragged nightie and thick glasses that gave her a bird-like aspect. As she voraciously rummaged through a carton of old clothes, I wandered around the house noting the chipped and broken things and an altar with frames of Zarathustra, Shiva and Parvati. In the unkempt yard, I saw the boy Burjor, playing with rustic toys as his mother darned clothes and the old man stretched out on an armchair on the verandah. Burjor wheeled his wooden lorry over to the verandah crawling on soiled hands and knees, down the plinth on which his mother sat, up her diligent arm and bent head and then down her back, ridged by shoulder blades exposed by her low blouse, turning left towards the armchair, driving up the wooden leg, making a death-defying leap to the arm and then negotiating the uneven surface of his father's reposing hand, the bony knoll of the ulna, the furry pelt, the wide curve of a solid shoulder. It was the monsoon, the rains had turned the mud roads to pudding, which meant that Burjor's father, Mr Elavia, was bound in Vansda for months. Miles away in Navsari, his wife suffered in the knowledge he was with his mistress. Every year whetted her fury, whose keen edge Burjor felt as a school-going boy living in his father's home in Navsari.

On returning to Bombay, I wrote a piece on my trip for the weekend edition. It was published with pictures I'd taken of the families in their sorry village homes. Mahrukh Marolia, the unofficial spokesperson for Parsi zealots, objected since the issue of mixed race Parsis was a touchy one for the orthodoxy, and Daniel Chacko wavered between wanting to please her and to run a good story. But Adi steered the piece through.

"Now you've become a hotshot journalist or what?" Mahrukh said. "Thinks she's Mother Teresa."

Soon after the article was out, the Zapsters were flooded with offers of donations. Homi, like a proud parent on a child's graduation day, organized a small gathering of the Adhkachru Club to celebrate. We met at a dive in Fort, where the seafood was good. There was Eruch, the shrewd peon, now the chief of the administration department in a company; Piloo, the pickle lady; Jal, a contractor; Neville, a yoga teacher; Bapsi, who oversaw the kitchen in an NGO that makes and sells Parsi food and turned out, according to Piloo, the best dal ni pori in the city; Homi and me. Imelda came too. She knew some of the Adhkachrus for she'd got a couple of them jobs in the liquor business. "Hello, my kachha-pukka friends," she said. I invited Hilla and Jimmy Kapadia, who, having few opportunities to meet new people after retiring, jumped at my call.

The mood was immediately convivial. They quickly got down to ribbing each other and swapping stories. No one seemed to find it strange that I was in their midst and they spoke of Burjor as though I'd always been privy to his life. Only I felt the delicious weirdness of the situation, of receiving great affection from strangers for being Burjor ni dikri, the daughter of Burjor, as Homi had introduced me.

Drinks and snacks were ordered. Bottles of beer, quarters of whisky and rum, fresh lime soda. Homi, with showy indulgence, ordered several plates of fried fish (freshly loaded with funds, ZAP was footing the tab): batter-fried prawn, Bombay Duck, mandeli, lep, surmai stuffed with chutney. Neville, who was vegetarian, snacked on a plate of lurid gobi Manchurian. "This Adhkachru eats kachra only," someone said.

The place was filling with office-goers, there to have a couple of drinks before heading home. Their low-level hum of conversation was interrupted by our lively table.

Pilamai, how's the pickle business?

Good, but not as masaledaar as your life. (Jal had recently acquired a mistress.)

Keep it down!

Oh, everyone knows, even your wife.

How would she know?

Women smell these things.

Then why hasn't she said anything?

Maybe she's having an affair of her own!

Imelda, queen of aunty bars is being an aunty and avoiding daru. (Imelda had ordered the fresh lime soda.)

So should you, fatso.

Look at Eruch's stomach. He used to be so thin and handsome.

Only Homi is fit.

Because he's not married. He doesn't have a wife to feed him, bugger does everything himself. Still stuck on that con job Meher.

Homi is a one-woman man. Unlike our friend Burjor, who was a ladies' man. No offence, Maya. All the girls in the colony were crazy about him.

Except my Hilla.

That's what you think, Jimmy.

How do you know what goes on in my head?

He seduced my only daughter. Because of him, she left me and went away to Canada. She's a fool but being older, he should've kept his hands off. Sorry, Maya. He didn't, but I still helped him escape when I could have put him in jail, for the sake of all the women he fucked over. I don't care about that bava he killed.

27

Phiroze and his rabid crew had it out for Burjor ever since he'd bloodied Cyrus's face for vandalizing his cab. Their simmering hatred for Burjor was stirred by his wealth, which he made a half-hearted attempt to hide. The guy was fond of good clothes, he wore a chunky watch, he was busy, having the air of a man occupied with moving up in life. Men like Cyrus and Phiroze were rough, mean-spirited, resenting the success of others but without the ambition to rise above their own positions. They reconnoitred Burjor jealously, waiting for a chance to somehow trip him.

They noticed the people who came to meet Burjor. They were ordinary-looking men and women, not the kind of people who'd visit a smuggler. And the women were definitely not jilted lovers like Philomena Braganza and Hufrish Desai. Phiroze and his thugs smelt opportunity, sniffed a whiff of a dubious scheme aside from the smuggling racket. How to uncover it? Engaging Homi, Burjor's taciturn lieutenant with lupine eyes, was pointless. He looked hostile, capable of violence despite his spindly frame. Perhaps he was Burjor's hatchet man. If you ran a smuggling racket, you were bound to have cutthroats on your rolls.

"I had a look that said if you come near me, I'll give you one," Homi said, miming the action of punching someone in the face.

So Phiroze, the chief sleuth in this operation, took it upon himself to subtly interrogate the people coming to see Burjor. He had time on his hands. Hilla's parents, who'd once wanted him for their son-in-law, had been sure Phiroze would pass the chartered accountancy examination and get a good job. But he failed and was disinclined to take it again. He got a low-level accounting job but was asked to leave not long after he joined, when employees complained of his temper and bullying ways. At the time he launched the operation to unmask Burjor, he was unemployed and broke. The others in Phiroze's group could only participate in speculative conversations in the evenings and weekends when the gang convened in the compound to ogle at girls and heckle those they found amusing.

"Every time I walked by, Phiroze would pass some dirty comment. 'Look at that fat ass. If she wants to punish Jimmy, she just has to sit on him.' And what not," Hilla said.

The rest of the time, they were at work. Cyrus, Phiroze's closest chum, spent as much time as he could away from the colony. Once he was done with work at the typewriter factory, where he was a mechanic, he would hit the gym. Not the one near the colony, where Burjor and Phiroze exercised, but one that was a short bus ride away. By the time he got home, the colony compound was vacant. People were in for the night, and there was little risk of running into Armaity. As he walked to his ground floor flat, Cyrus would resist the urge to look up at Armaity and Burjor's open window in the building across.

"How do you know he avoided looking up at their window?" I asked Hilla.

"That's my masala to the story. But it's believable."

"Hilla aunty, let's stick to what you actually know."

"Then what's the fun ya?"

The sight of Armaity, who seemed lovelier than ever after marriage, caused him intense suffering. Hilla's theory was that Cyrus saw Armaity as some kind of redemption. She could have, with her goodness, lifted him out of the quicksand life of Naval Baug, the deathly tug of his wicked gang and difficult father. The old man, Boman, was a singular unit of vice. A drunk and a gambler, he lived off Cyrus and the meagre winnings he made at the gambling den across the road. When he was broke, he would sell things from the house. Cyrus would often come home to find a couch or a new radio missing. Anything he wanted to preserve would have to be locked in a steel cupboard. Once he was careless with the keys, leaving them exposed. When he returned from work, he found the cupboard open and missing a new watch he'd purchased with a half a month's salary. Boman had used it to pay a gambling debt. That night father and son had fought loudly enough for half the colony to hear. Boman went too far when he sold Cyrus's Yezdi not long after the fight with Burjor.

"If you said to him, 'The world's coming to an end. You get to save either Boman or the Yezdi', he would pick his bike," Jimmy said.

Every weekend, Cyrus would clean and oil the bike with his slender yet firm mechanic's hands. He would go on a biking holiday once a year with friends and cousins; they'd been to Rajasthan, all the way to Kanyakumari. When Boman sold the Yezdi, Cyrus began to stealthily find a way to leave Naval Baug. Some months later, he moved to Bangalore, to join a cousin's bike repair shop.

"We heard he mellowed down, married a Madrasi, had children," Hilla said. "He never called Boman, didn't even come for his funeral."

Boman, who'd been sure that Cyrus's threats to leave were empty, was beside himself. Naturally, he didn't blame himself but sought a target. After a period of drunken speculation, aided by his no-good friends in the gambling den across Naval Baug, Boman made Burjor the culprit. Burjor had publicly humiliated Cyrus and stolen his girl, driving him away and depriving his old father of a livelihood.

Boman's fury was fanned every time he saw Armaity and Burjor together, which was often. Keeping a romance under wraps in Naval Baug was almost impossible, and after a point, the lovers stopped trying to still wagging tongues. He'd take her around town in his Ambassador taxi, to the movies, to show her parts of the city he liked. It gave them a kick, Hilla said, to see the surprised looks on the faces of people on the street as they passed by. Here was a cabbie, who looked too good to be one, and a stylish woman by his side. Armaity with her pale Persian skin and chic dresses that she had stitched—her preferred style was the shirt dress, the fitted bodice and pencil skirt showing off her slim frame to excellent effect—must've appeared like an aristocrat sneaking off to explore the city. This was *Roman Holiday* playing out right here. They even gave up being furtive about their nightly assignations at Burjor's place. After Armaity's uncle and aunt passed, she had no one to answer to, which meant she could do exactly as she pleased. It was on one of these visits that Burjor knocked her up. Armaity found she was pregnant only three months later. Two bloodless months aroused no suspicion for her period had always been erratic.

"It was the end of their honeymoon period," said Hilla, who re-entered Burjor's orbit around the time he and Armaity were seeing each other. She and Jimmy had withdrawn themselves, wary of whatever shady activities Burjor was involved with. Needing a friend to confide in, someone who knew Burjor well, Armaity courted Hilla, reeling her back into their lives.

Armaity, thinking her errant ovaries would deny her children, was ecstatic. This also meant Burjor would have to marry her, a proposal she'd made in subtle ways that he'd wilfully ignored. She had hoped, Hilla said, that Burjor would want a stable family life after his miserable childhood, but this was not the case.

"I don't know from where she got the idea," Homi said. "Burjor was a free spirit always, he never wanted to be tied down. We hated our fathers for putting us in this situation, you know. My thinking is that he didn't want to ruin some kid's life because he knew he could not give himself hundred per cent. I was the opposite. I wanted a wife and babies but it never worked out."

They had a hurried wedding and Armaity moved in. Immediately, she established herself as the householder, taking charge of the kitchen, cleaning up the mess of bachelorhood. Far from being pleased, Burjor chafed against this new form of control. He stayed away for long hours and grudgingly took her out on weekends. His attitude didn't help Armaity's difficult pregnancy.

A slender woman, she had rapidly gained weight. Her feet and arms were swollen, even her face. Her blood pressure spiralled and the doctor advised her bed rest. I imagined her lying prone on the bed in a nightie, her feet raised, her beauty inflated to grotesque proportions, waiting for her husband to come home and show her some tenderness. But he was rarely home, which meant Armaity had to cook, dust and shop. By then, they could afford a cleaner, who came daily to sweep and swab. On days she felt ill, she commissioned Jermai, who lived in the widows' chawl in Naval Baug and who'd couriered messages between Burjor and Hufrish

Desai, to buy groceries. And then one day, the thing she feared came to pass. While soaking his soiled clothes, she smelt an unfamiliar scent on Burjor's shirt, Eau de Cologne. Burjor wore a musky, masculine perfume, one of the colognes he smuggled into the country.

"That was Philomena," Imelda Braganza said.

Even after the scene she'd created at the colony, Philomena and Burjor had kept in touch. She was too much in love with him to cut off contact. And because he enjoyed having a cloud of women he could call on when he needed, a comforting cushion of feminine compassion, he reeled her back by apologizing. Once again, she demanded he marry her only to hear the same non-committal noises.

The two would meet at the Dhobi Talao house she shared with her mother when Imelda was out. Naturally, Imelda found out; she was informed by watchful neighbours. It was a stupid thing to do but then Philomena, Imelda said, was "mental over Burjor".

"I gave her one slap and told her you fool, you actually think he's going to leave his wife for you? He didn't want to marry her and she looks like a bloody bombshell. You think he wants you? I don't know who is the bigger chootiya, him or you," Imelda said.

Imelda's blow destroyed once and for all Burjor's seductive grip over her and sent Philomena hurtling into the arms of her future husband, the man who would soon take her to Canada.

"Basically, it was good for his ego to have many

options," Imelda said. "After Philly went and embarrassed herself, Burjor got in touch, not her. You see what I'm saying? He liked to have the power to give and take, the rascal."

The Eau de Cologne could even have been Mini's (who still wears the stuff) had she allowed Burjor to touch her. It was about the time of their ambiguous friendship. Burjor, pretending to be a cabbie, playing truant from business, driving Mini to college, taking her out for meals.

"Jesus, when did he have time to run all his businesses between these women?" I said, rattled that my father juggled women with such dexterity.

"He had his chief minister, our Homi," Imelda said. "Bugger was like any other man, didn't want responsibility. Bhenchod."

Such was Burjor's aversion to his pregnant wife that when he wasn't with one of his women or working, he would secrete himself in Eruch Amrolia's library. Eruch worked as an accountant at State Bank of India. He was a gangly fellow with eyes magnified by thick glasses, an Adam's apple like an iceberg and one arm shorter than the other. The colony bullies, who got a kick out of applying nicknames to eccentrics and the handicapped, called him Thunio, the stunted. He spoke little unless you got him started on his heroes, Einstein and Galileo. Then he wouldn't stop till you lied saying you had to leave. His parents had to live with pictures of scientists taped to the walls of their living room. They could never get used to Einstein sticking his tongue out at them as they braced for the day with their morning mint tea and khari biscuits. When he entered the colony, his long bony legs sticking out like trophy handles from either side of his Bajaj scooter, Phiroze and gang would call out: Aye Thunio, aye aapro Einstein ayo. Aye Thunio, our Einstein has come.

Amrolia's tiny apartment was filled with books and magazines on science, history, current affairs. From his book-lined grotto in the village of Naval Baug, Eruch looked out onto the world. Similarly for Burjor, Eruch's library was a telescope showing him the universe beyond the colony. It was from here that Burjor had either purloined or borrowed the copy of *National Geographic* in my inherited carton. The issue's cover story was on Nepal and the solitary heights of the Himalayas, which would have seemed like the greatest escape from earthly duties. I imagined Burjor and Eruch reading in companionable silence as, across the colony, Armaity, lonely and suffering a precarious pregnancy, moved her bulk slowly around the apartment.

28

Not long after my article on ZAP was published, things began to go badly at work. It was the time of the year we were given raises. No matter how profitable the paper was, we were told the same excuse. The market was bad, targets had not been achieved, hence employees could expect only a minor rise in pay. What I did not expect was to be told, by Daniel Chacko, my invertebrate boss, that I had performed far below expectations because of which I would get no promotion even though I was due for one and just a five per cent raise. He delivered this appraisal solemn-faced but the fact that he refused to meet my eyes suggested an ulterior design.

"What the fuck, Daniel. You know I'm one of the few people on the desk with real language skills. Your new lot of editors don't know a comma from a semicolon. I'm the last of the fucking Mohicans."

"That's your other problem, insubordination. You can't use such language with me," Chacko said.

The ones who did well at the paper were Chacko's favourites, chief among them Mahrukh Marolia. Adi

Sanjana had retired as front-page editor and Mahrukh was elevated in his place. Immediately, she began reorganizing the newsroom, establishing herself as a petty chieftain. A base creature with a limited view of the world, Mahrukh was puffed up because her first position of real power allowed her to mess around with the careers of people she disliked. "She must've been one of those kids who dismembered insects for fun," Tumpa had once observed about her. Not long after her promotion, I was summoned to Chacko's office. Mahrukh was there, trying but failing to subdue the look of a lion that has cornered a gazelle. Beaming suspiciously, Chacko told me the paper was starting a new edition in Baroda for which they were hiring. Mahrukh had a tremendous idea, Chacko said. Why not send an experienced editor like Maya to set it up?

"The other day, you were complaining about not getting a promotion," Chacko said. "Today, I'm giving you a double promotion."

"A punishment posting to the boondocks. This is your idea of a carrot?"

"Maya, you'll be the editor of an edition," Mahrukh said, feigning disbelief.

"In Baroda, where excitement occurs only when kids at the art university exhibit nude paintings that bring the right-wing to their gates."

"You know your contract says you can expect to be posted to any edition in the country," Chacko said. "Sleep over it."

Tumpa had recently quit to join the India bureau of the online edition of a major American paper, leaving me without an accessible confidant—and smarting with jealousy over her success.

"Boss, treat this as a blessing in disguise and put in your papers. Otherwise you'll never leave, being the darpok that you are," Tumpa said, when I told her about Mahrukh and Chacko's scheme to punish me. For what? For writing an article that pissed Mahrukh off? For improving her crudely written stories?

"We've always known Chacko is a choot," Tumpa said.

Far for being upset, Mini and Shivaji were equally relieved. They too thought that Chacko's offer could be the spur I needed to leave the paper.

"Why aren't you telling me to get another job before quitting this one? That's the wise thing to do," I asked Mini. We were on the balcony smoking a spliff of some terrific weed Kersi had procured from a fellow who grew the stuff near Goa. Kersi and I were no longer lovers. He'd called it off, not wanting to do the no-strings-attached thing anymore. Either we started seeing each other or limited our meetings to scoring stuff till he succeeded in quelling his feelings for me. I'd disappointed him by readily agreeing. Though I missed the comforting temperature of his body, which radiated heat like a warm kettle, and our weekend jaunts around the city.

"I know you," Mini said. "You'll procrastinate over

finding another job and in the meantime, accept the Baroda assignment."

The rest of the week was spent in fearful contemplation of leaving the womb-like asylum of the paper, where I'd worked for ten years. There would be a period of unemployment and an anxious search for a job. Would I be able to survive in a different ether? Carry out a job that posed bigger challenges, as any job other than this no doubt would? The thought of giving up my lovable routine was terrifying. Spending the morning leisurely reading the newspapers over breakfast, occasionally exercising, arriving at the office in the early afternoon, proceeding straightaway for lunch in the canteen, editing mundane reports, observing the daily pageant of newsroom life... Was I ready to renounce the spectacle of Purnendu striding around the office cursing in Bengali, casting prurient glances at women? Or cathartic discussions with Bengali colleagues on our alimentary troubles? Or rambling conversations with Saint Thomas? Or the kick of being in a newsroom electrified by a major event? Or the saccharine lemon tea dispensed by the crud-encrusted machine? Things that were hateful suddenly seemed charming. Once again, I was assailed by the familiar feeling of dizziness that prefaced an unknown quantity. And I imagined walking by the side of my lifelong guide Kierkegaard, skipping to keep up with the slight, swift-paced man as he marched erratically on the pavement, dodging patches of sunlight to keep to the shade. Waving his cane dangerously as he spoke, he advised me to take the leap, overcome my anxiety to create new meaning for myself or I would be forever guilty.

After a week of hectic reflection and a sustained campaign by Mini to "grow some balls", I told Chacko I was quitting. Having pegged me as a lifer at the paper, Chacko was taken aback. Not wanting to lose a good editor at a time the desk badly needed experienced hands, he said I didn't have to worry about being sent to Baroda. And he'd see whether the paper could improve my raise. It was as if I'd called his bluff. The offer was tempting, but Chacko's pathetic about-turn—in fact, I felt enraged on Mahrukh's behalf; the guy didn't have the guts to stay true to his loyal lieutenant—made it easier to quit.

On my last day at the paper, the folks at work took me to the Press Club for farewell drinks. Having attended several such occasions, I knew exactly where the evening was headed. There would be an initial period of awkwardness as not all of us were used to hanging out after work. Purnendu aka Boomba, Chacko and the Bengali boys often drank at the club after putting an edition to bed; women were never part of these soirees. Greased by alcohol, the stilted small talk would slide into loose-tongued, borderline inappropriate conversation that could, if not restrained in time, skid further into a trading of insults or baldly offensive assaults. Usually, Adi Sanjana, the former front-page editor, acted as the sentry, reigning in Purnendu and

Chacko, who smashed their filters after three stiff whiskies, unleashing outrageous and obscene thoughts normally caged by sobriety. But Sanjana, who had retired recently, declined to attend even though he'd been fond of me. Instead Mahrukh, who had been elevated to Sanjana's position, showed up.

Now Mahrukh rarely attended Press Club dos. She and Purnendu had a longstanding enmity. He was of the opinion (rightly so) that she had become a substandard reporter and, being from Calcutta, found her Bombay-bred writing to be childlike and full of errors (which was true). The sight of Purnendu pulling Mahrukh up for her writing, he at his computer pointing out gaps in reportage and bad grammar ("What do you have against articles, dammit!"), she looking over his shoulder at her errant copy, fuming at being embarrassed before the newsroom, was a common one. Mahrukh often asked Chacko to intervene, a situation he dreaded for it meant mediating between his drinking buddy and his front-page story mill (even though he was as appalled as Purnendu at her writing, being from Kerala, a state where the standard of instruction is higher than that of Maharashtra). Mahrukh, however, was convinced that Purnendu was after her because he was jealous of her success (she had three times the Twitter followers he did) and because she was fat. She was certain that Purnendu found her healthy proportions (her words to describe her generous frame, not mine), disgusting (he did, it's true) and used her stories as an excuse to punish her for her girth (untrue). The point is that Mahrukh came for my farewell knowing full well the risk of Purnendu getting drunk and saying hurtful things about her appearance, which he eventually did because he was too drunk for anything other than a vicious personal attack.

Why then did Mahrukh attend? Because she was tempted by the delicious possibility of drama. Purnendu was annoyed with me for leaving for it meant one less hand on the desk. The younger sub-editors drove Purnendu up the wall with their mistakes ("They don't know the difference between a colon and semicolon, bhenchod!"). Ever since I broke the news to him, he'd been edgy with me.

"Where are you going, tell me," he had said, loud enough for half the newsroom to hear.

"Nowhere, I swear I haven't got another job. I just want to take it easy for a while."

"Take it easy? Take it easy! You're so rich you can afford to take it easy! Is it a boy? No it can't be. Ato constipation. Padh mere mere chhelera ke mere phelbi." You're so constipated, you'd kill boys with your farts.

"Ja, ekta Lomotil kheye ne. Tor verbal diarrhoea ta bondo hoye jabe." Go take a Lomotil. Your verbal diarrhoea will stop.

"If you write a memoir—let's assume you do something with your life—you know what you should call it? Paadher Panchali. Ay, Shomshuddho! Shoonli, Maya's writing a book about her life called Paadher

Panchali." Shomshuddho (his crony), did you hear? Maya's writing a book called the Song of Her Farts.

Now Mahrukh, who lacked the subtle cellular antennae needed to read situations, mistook Purnendu's gassy jabs for real bile. The guy was fond of me in his own way, we were bound by a common language and an obsession with alimentary movements. I tolerated his baser observations (about my skinny frame that had no meat to hang on to) since it was difficult to take him seriously, an odd-looking, clownish fellow whose wolfish act evaporated before tough women. (He was lamb-like with his wife around.) Other women who'd overhead his obscene appraisals of them for the benefit of his Bengali coterie had complained to Chacko, who had, obviously, done nothing to improve his pal.

So Mahrukh, oblivious of our dynamic despite having worked in the same office for years, showed up at the Press Club salivating at the thought of a showdown. The evening began expectedly with awkward conversation over booze and snacks, fried okra, named after a veteran film journalist, a stir-fry of boiled black chickpeas called Chana in China, and chicken tikka. Purnendu and Chacko were drinking whisky like water, I was sipping gin and tonic, alert for signs of danger. Next to me Tumpa, who had been invited since the two of us were friends, was buzzed on rum and coke. By the time Mahrukh arrived, Purnendu was on his third whisky. She ordered jal jeera, the cumin-flavoured drink known for its laxative properties. I saw that Purnendu, smirking, had noticed and knew right then that he was going to crack shit jokes.

After twenty minutes of chatting about front-page fuck-ups, the latest political exigency, fresh gossip on the publisher, Tumpa, who had been missing our flatulent chatter, said, "Boombada, beshi chana kheyo na. Shara raat gas hobe." Go easy on the chana, you'll fart all night.

"Tumpa, I've been seeing the gas you've been writing. Think you're very smart, working for a foreign bureau?"

"It's the real shit, Boombada. What I was doing here was gas."

"You know who's not very smart?" Mahrukh chimed in. "Maya, for giving up such a good opportunity. It's not too late baba. No, Chacko?"

She was drunk on cumin water, calling me baba, an endearment I'd never heard her use with anyone, let alone me.

"The offer's open Maya," Chacko said, droopy-eyed between his third and fourth large whisky. "Baroda, Bombay, whatever."

"Not Bombay, Chacko," Mahrukh said. "She'll grow slowly here. Just think of the scope in Baroda. You'll be running the edition. Next step, resident editor in one the major bureaus."

"After twenty years in that hick town," I said.

"Hick? What is hick?"

"Ay Tumpa," Purnendu said, shovelling Chana in China into his mouth. "Gondho pachhish? Parsi paadh." Can you smell the Parsi fart?

"Sali chicken kheyechhe mone hoy," Tumpa said. Seems like she had sali chicken.

"According to me, it's dhansak," said Debu, Purnendu's favourite toady.

"Guys, Boomba," Chacko warned, half-hearted.

"What's he saying?" Mahrukh said, her limited faculties finally sensing a malevolent current wafting her way from the other end of the table where Purnendu sat.

"He's saying you're farting," Tumpa said.

"What nonsense!"

"The amount of jal jeera you're having, you must be shitting in your pants," Purnendu said. "There'll be a skid mark or two at least. You know sometimes when you fart, a bit of shit comes out."

"Skid what? What's he saying?"

"He's saying your chuddies will have smears of potty," Tumpa said.

"The man is obsessed," Mahrukh said. "Just grow up."

"I'm obsessed because I have to clean shit at the paper every day. And you know whose is the toughest to clean? Yours, Mahrukh. A fat lot of shit comes out of your fat arse every day."

"Oh oh, this is outlandish! Chacko!" Mahrukh said.

"No Mahrukh, this is *outrageous*," Tumpa corrected.

"Akkebare primiteev," Purnendu said. She's primitive.

"What's he saying?" Mahrukh said, half rising, bristling in her floral shirt.

"I'm saying you're the worst kind of journalist. Lazy,

craven, corrupt. You're the corrosive crud wrecking the system each time you write a biased story that you, bastard (turning to Chacko), insist on carrying, or take a favour in exchange for PR in the paper. I want to (gritting his teeth and making a scooping motion with his hand) scrape you off with a spatula."

"What, what!" Mahrukh, breathless.

"Don't understand? Go look up a dictionary or ask your ten thousand Twitter followers. 'Twitterverse, what does crud mean? Hashtag havingablondemoment'."

"Purnendu, bas kar yaar, stop it," Chacko said, his drunken head lolling on his chest.

"Ay you shut up chootiya," Purnendu said. "Look at this gandu, babbling after four drinks. No capacity for alcohol or integrity."

"You're no revolutionary, bhenchod," Chacko slurred. "Thinks he's still a Calcutta commie."

"Enough of this nonsense. I'm going to take this unacceptable behaviour up with HR. Actually, forget HR, I'm going straight to the top. Chacko, I've warned you," Mahrukh said and, manoeuvring her cumin-watered bulk out of the chair, marched out of the bar.

"Ay Tumpa, at last we can breathe na? Parsi paadh gulo deadly." Parsi farts are deadly.

"Boss..." I said, overcome with affection.

—

Soon after leaving, I threw myself into writing the chapter on Burjor for Karela's book for it helped to fill the void caused by leaving the paper. Being at home at four in the afternoon, a time when I'd be in the thick of the newsroom's swirl, was a discombobulating sensation. Karela provided a distraction by finally introducing me to the publisher of his book, a fellow called Jamshed Shroff, and I was keen to see him again.

There were two reasons for this. A youthful forty-year-old, Jamshed had, like many Parsis, inherited a vast sum of money from deceased, childless relatives. He'd been moderately wealthy in his own right as a manufacturer of poker equipment, a business he sold immediately after receiving his bequest. (He then made a nick in his fortune by travelling for the most part of a year and, Karela said with a snigger, dallying with a series of "high maintenance" women, one as young as twenty.) In his spare time—he had a lot of it—Jamshed played poker with various groups. There was a gang from Cusrow Baug, largely unemployed men who played low stakes poker. Jamshed called them "enjoyers of life". The high stakes guys were industrialists, sons of politicians and bankers. And there were a couple mid-range clubs. Not many knew that even though Jamshed had Parsi parents, he hadn't been given a navjote as his mother had, some time before his seventh birthday, converted to Christianity and, intoxicated by religious fervour, forbidden a navjote for her son. She'd wanted Jamshed to convert too but his father had objected. Years later, disenchanted with her adopted faith, Mrs Shroff began visiting fire temples again and wearing a sadra-kusti.

She regretted not getting Jamshed's navjote done, but by then it was too late.

"I'm an Adhkachru, like you," he said.

Like me, he was after meaning. Shroff was using a part of his fortune to fund a digital news site. At the time, there were a couple of cultural web magazines but no fully digital news publication other than those by the dailies. According to Karela, who occasionally played poker with the Cusrow Baug group, Jamshed was embarrassed over his sudden wealth and, therefore, keen to spend it on something worthwhile. A business head and an editor, who I knew by reputation, had been found. They were putting together a bureau and Jamshed had casually asked if I was interested in editing the site's culture section. It was mainly to pursue this offer that I was eager to see the guy.

There was also another, baser motive. Not since my jejune romance with Danish Khan had I met a man with the brain-melting quality Jamshed had. It wasn't so much his looks; in fact, his close-set eyes gave him a maniacal appearance. He had an aura of authority, he radiated a capacity to get things done. This had an aphrodisiac effect on me. And despite his sophistication (everything he wore was custom-made), there was a nefarious whiff about him, possibly a projection of my own imagination fired by Karela's description.

"Calm your hormones the fuck down," Tumpa said, when we spoke. "The man sounds like a dabbler, a dilettante. Who knows if he has the stamina for anything long-term? I'm talking about both relationships and this new project of his. Remember, rich folks have nothing to lose."

The first time we met was on the street at the back of the Taj hotel in Colaba. Karela and I had walked from his place at Oval Maidan, discussing the book on the way. Jamshed, who lived in the area, met us at the start of the street and walked with us till Mereweather Road before disappearing into one of the buildings. Along the way, he shook hands with or waved to practically every seller of Kashmiri shawls and phoney antiques, every parking attendant and even a vagrant.

"Got to make friends with the high and the low," he said.

I was reminded of Burjor. In my fevered imagination, Jamshed had the same savvy, the hustler's cockiness. That first meeting suggested he had the dominating quality I sought in men. This was the reason, I had concluded, none of the men I'd been with had swept me off my feet. They were too accommodating. Imagine that! What sort of sick mind did I have! Jamshed, on the other hand, gave me a once-over and said with seductive derision, "It's true, journalists dress like shit."

"It's called shabby chic," I said, feeling gauche, Tramp to his Lady.

"You look as chic as my watchman."

Once Jamshed left, Karela turned to me with a stern look.

"Don't even think about it. The man is bad news," he said.

"What are you talking about?"

"You think I didn't see the way you were looking at him? There were stars in your eyes. I'm warning you, Jamshed's a player."

"Where did you learn that youthful word, old man?"

"I spend time with people below me in age. They keep me young."

29

During Armaity's pregnancy, Burjor ceased running the employment agency from Naval Baug, moving operations to the warehouse in Wadi Bunder, a portion of which he rented to store smuggled stuff. Phiroze had kept up a malicious campaign against Burjor, making people who'd been unconcerned about his activities fearful that he was up to something dangerous. Now an invisible sign hovered above Burjor marking him a grave threat. After all his efforts to gather intelligence, Phiroze finagled the truth, not from one of the fifty-fifties, but from Jermai, the old widow, who ran errands for Armaity. Crafty Jermai, always on the lookout for ways to make money and earn some food, was easy to bribe. In return for a dozen eggs, she agreed to tune into the conversations of the Elavia household and pass on the intelligence to Phiroze.

Phiroze was over the moon, this was dynamite. He spread the word and overnight, the entire colony knew that Burjor had mixed blood (this explained the toffee hue of his skin) and that he was helping his kind get jobs in the city. The colony was divided. There were the progressive folk, who admired Burjor's ingenuity, and there were the rednecks, repulsed by the idea of mixed Parsis. Some of the older ones had written furious letters to a Parsi weekly during the controversy over the navjote of 1942. Hilla and Jimmy were cornered by groups belonging to both factions and interrogated.

"Oh my god, overnight we became the most popular people in the colony," Hilla said. "The old fogeys were hopping mad. They said we'll write letters to all the papers, we'll put an end to this, our blood is being contaminated and what not."

Armaity, waddling out of the apartment, for a walk—she should've been in bed with her feet up but being indoors all day was unbearable—immediately noticed a shift in the currents of the colony's atmosphere. Her neighbours gave her stilted smiles, two women in the compound whispered to each other while looking at her. Jermai, walking to her home carrying bags of leftovers, couldn't look her in the eye. Perturbed, Armaity walked to a phone booth and dialled Hilla at work, at the Fort branch of State Bank of India, and got the story.

According to Homi, the episode disrupted Burjor's general monkish equilibrium, bringing back memories of the ignominy he'd known as a kid in Navsari living with a stepmother, who treated him like a serf. (He wasn't one to talk about his feelings but on this occasion, he confided in Homi.) Phiroze, who'd been angling for a confrontation ever since Burjor had shoved him off

Jimmy, now watched, like a leopard crouching in the grass waiting for a chance to spring on an idling deer, for a suitable chance to start a fight.

"Can you imagine being married to this guy?" Hilla said. "His whole life was about bringing people down."

"Where is he now?"

"In a sanatorium in Navsari. Alzheimer's got to him some years back. He would step out of the house and lose his way. They would find him in all kinds of places. Once he got into a train and ended up in Thana. The kids in the colony called him Gando, mad. As a young man, he would call other people names. Now it was his turn."

One evening, as Burjor entered the colony after work, Phiroze and his cronies called him a dubra as he walked by. In the past, when they'd taken digs at him for his scenes with Hufrish and Philomena, Burjor had ignored them. This time, he answered back, handing Phiroze the opportunity he was after. (Jimmy and half the colony watched from their balconies.) Words were exchanged and the two parties, Burjor alone on one hand and Phiroze and his pack on the other, moved closer, firing impulses to their fists and feet to prepare for a skirmish. The colony inhaled. But at that very moment, unfortunately for Phiroze, Eruch Amrolia flew into the compound on his scooter and, near the cluster of opponents, braked suddenly when a kid on a cycle shot into his path from one side. Eruch knocked the cycle over and the kid fell, grazing his arm. His mother, one of the spectators that evening, shrieked and ran down to the compound to comfort her son and lightly cuff Eruch on the arm even though he was not the one at fault. Phiroze lost his chance as the colony's attention shifted to Eruch, the injured child and his furious mother.

"But I knew that something was going to happen hundred per cent," Jimmy said.

It happened in the gym some days later. The two clashed when Phiroze went up to Burjor, who was either lifting weights or doing squats, and in a mocking tone asked for a job. He'd been unemployed for months. Could Burjor find him work? Or did he absolutely have to be a dubra to qualify? He wasn't eligible just because his father hadn't fucked an adivasi? That wasn't fair. Then Phiroze got what he wanted. Burjor leapt at him and the two went down brutalizing each other for many minutes till they were prised apart by others.

"How did Armaity take this?" I asked Hilla.

"She was very disturbed. She was afraid all the negative energy around would affect the child."

For weeks after the bust-up with Phiroze, Armaity felt that the colony reverberated with a rancorous pulse. It was as if the Elavias were being punished for doing something illegal, and she had the irrational fear that cops would one day show up at their door. All kinds of rumours went around, some deliberately started by Phiroze. Burjor was enlisting fifty-fifties to man his flotilla of smuggling boats so that he could swiftly rival operators like Haji Mastan. He was amassing an army of fifty-fifties in order to one day threaten the Parsi dispensation and pollute the Zoroastrian bloodline. If his plan came to pass, Parsis would lose their distinctiveness, their fair skin, noble Iranian noses, philanthropic spirit, business brains.

"What business brain, bhenchod?" Homi said. "Burjor had a business brain. Those colonywallahs were all clerks and workers."

Jangled by the colony's hostile tremors, Armaity stopped going out altogether. Imelda Braganza, who despite Burjor's shameful behaviour with her daughter, stayed in touch, began visiting Armaity three times a week with groceries and tasty food. It was equally strange that Burjor didn't hesitate to ask Imelda to look after Armaity. At the time, Philomena had recently met her future husband. She'd quickly decided to marry him and move to Canada, far from the magnetic pull of her ex and a mother who loved the ex like a son.

It was during one of Imelda's visits—she'd come bearing potato chops and plum cake—that Armaity's water broke. Imelda left word with Hilla, who was at work at the bank, and took Armaity to a nursing home.

"I remember standing on the road with your mother trying to get a taxi," Imelda said. "Our own taxiwallah was god knows where."

When Burjor arrived, Armaity was hysterical with pain. A nagging discomfort beneath her ribs during her pregnancy, a feeling she'd diagnosed as flatulence, had intensified to such a degree she felt her insides were being gored by needles. The doctor privately told Burjor her life was at risk and that she had to deliver immediately. She had a severe case of HELLP, which meant her liver was dangerously swollen. A test revealed she was bleeding internally. But she seemed fine throughout the pregnancy, Burjor said. How could she suddenly be on the brink of death?

"She had high blood pressure but maybe the doctor wasn't attentive enough or something or maybe Armaity didn't get check-ups as often as she should have, I don't know," Imelda said. "Remember, it was a difficult time for the girl. There was a lot going on in her head."

Armaity was given a blood transfusion and I was extracted from my amniotic enclave by way of a Caesarean section. She didn't make it.

Burjor, who could always be relied upon to get you out of a crisis, was for the first time helpless. There was no time to grieve. Who would take care of the kid? Who would breastfeed her? At a loss for answers, he allowed himself to be led by the women, Hilla and Imelda. Coincidentally, a woman in Naval Baug had recently given birth. It was known that she produced so much milk, she'd pump the excess into the sink. On Hilla's request, she began bottling her surfeit milk for me, and so for months I was fed in this way until Burjor, through his smuggling contacts, procured a breast milk substitute from the US. Forced to work from home, Burjor applied himself to taking care of his infant daughter. Hilla would babysit after work and on weekends, and Imelda stayed for days at a stretch to look after me, angering Philomena. Traitorous Jermai was recruited once more, on a generous salary, as a nanny. Burjor knew it was a bad idea but there was no time to find a better candidate.

30

I had naively thought that learning about Burjor would cure me of the weightlessness I felt, lower my centre of gravity. Instead I felt airier than ever. It drove me up the wall to think that the most eventful period in my life occurred at an age when only memories, no more complex than the sound of familiar voices, were recorded. Since I was working from home, I would frequently extract the carton from its place in my cupboard and handle the objects, imagining the feel of the sadra's stiff muslin or the metallic coolness of the Ricoh which would unlock memories of events seen by my infant eyes.

Meanwhile Shivaji, through his proxy Mini was attempting to bring me down to earth. The two of them—Shivaji, seriously, Mini, half-heartedly—thought I should think of marrying.

"He put an ad in the matrimonial section of the paper," Mini said, giggling. "Tall, fair, intelligent with good job from a simple family. Father in service, mother a college teacher."

"I don't have a job."

"We've got some decent responses. You should take a look."

"You can tell Shivaji he doesn't need to compensate for being an indifferent parent."

"I too want to see you well settled."

The amnesia of parents. Mini's marriage had been a disaster, she'd counselled countless friends through their own terrible partnerships. Yet, she missed the irony of suggesting marriage to me.

"I'm not feeling it."

"What does that mean? Speak English."

"It means I don't want to marry. Everything I've seen of the practice, including your own fucked up relationship, tells me it's a bad idea. Either your husband turns out to be a jerk or domesticity grinds the passion out of your life. I don't want to be tied down to a rotten apple or the routine of running a house, arguing over whose turn it is to do dishes."

"That's because you don't have to lift a finger here. Everything is done for you."

"You know what I mean."

"I hear the spirit of Burjor speaking through you."

I had been faithfully narrating the stories of Burjor I heard to Mini, who naturally viewed them through the lens of her own relationship with him. When she learned of the way he treated Armaity and Philomena, she felt a sense of vindication, that she'd been right to not pursue a relationship, even though Burjor, in all likelihood, wanted nothing more than a brief fling.

Tired of Mini's anxiety, I ushered her out of the room and got ready to go for a walk, needing the steadying hand of the city. On my way out, I crossed Shivaji, who ruffled my hair. If I'd stopped, he might have given me an awkward hug, an unfamiliar thing I wanted to avoid. So I slowed my stride as he brushed my scalp and sailed past before he could raise his other arm for a tentative embrace.

On my way down, I stopped at Kersi's for a quick smoke. We'd begun talking again though things were awkward between us. He had a new girlfriend, one of his yoga students, a very young Bengali like the last one.

"What's with you and Bong chicks?" I said.

"Don't know. Guess I'm attracted to brainy girls."

"The last one wasn't brainy. She and you thought she was, but she wasn't. What does this one do?"

"She's into event planning. Kids' birthday parties, weddings, conferences. That sort of thing."

"You don't need a brain for that."

"Don't be a choot, Maya."

It was strange to keep a stiff distance instead of sitting with my legs on his lap or in some other tactile position. I could sense that if I were to touch him in a meaningful way, he wouldn't resist. It was tempting because I missed Kersi's wiry body. But I kept my truant hands to myself remembering Burjor's behaviour with Philomena.

—

I was to meet Karela at Grant Road East. He wanted to walk from the station to Falkland Road to see the city's old cinema halls and beyond them, the remains of the red light district. He wanted to get a sense of the place to add colour to the final chapter in his book, a profile of the Irani owner of one of Bombay's most famous dance bars.

He was waiting at the bus stop on Grant Road bridge. From there, we walked to Falkland Road. These once classy theatres, which played Hollywood movies, were seedy yet terrifically atmospheric places where you could watch B-grade Hindi films and, apparently, get a hand-job for ten bucks. I'd read that the basement of each theatre contained the grave of an unknown saint. It was to see these funerary kernels that we first approached Alfred Cinema, which employed an old poster artist to hand-paint its hoardings. The watchman shooed us away, suspicious of anyone who looked they didn't belong to the area. Single men loitered in the lobby and a couple, excited by the sight of a foreign girl, danced near my elbow. Karela was charged up. Being there brought back memories of watching Hitchcock movies at the cinema with his parents and, as a young adult, visiting an opium den in the area for his first taste of the stuff. It wasn't often that he left the tranquil ether of the southern tip of Bombay. Here was chaos and strangeness, people seemed altered by a thrumming libidinal energy, whose source was a clutch of brothels further up the road. It made them heedless of propriety.

A man with paan-tinted teeth gave us directions, unsolicited, to the red light zone. "You want to see prostitutes?" he shouted.

"You know, in the last years of the nineteenth century, this place was the Ripon Theatre," Karela said. "It was Alfred later. Prostitutes got to watch movies at the special price of one rupee."

For thirty bucks, the caretaker at New Roshan Talkies next door, led us to the dusty, ramshackle area behind the hall where a movie was being shown. Steps led to the basement shrine containing a mausoleum covered with green velvet. It was here, infinitesimally closer to the earth's gravitational core, that I felt somewhat settled, the anxiety of weeks dispersing into the particulate environment of New Roshan's nether reaches.

We walked ahead towards the red light district, past one of the area's remaining Chinese dentists, whose clinic displayed moulds of teeth. There used to be many more Chinese, descendants of shippies who'd settled in India. Now a small number remained, the younger ones having migrated to Canada and Australia, the elders carrying on the old professions—dentistry, restaurants, beauty parlours.

"My father remembered seeing Chinese fellows smoking opium here," Karela said.

The red light area had dimmed. Housing complexes had come up where once middle-class folk wouldn't dream of living. They towered over the brothels, hellish blocks painted depressingly in bright colours, festooned with drying clothes, women and children. Nothing had mitigated prostitution like the housing crisis. Every inch of land was worth building on, forestland, slum acres, this historic plot of vice. This is a city in the service of real estate.

"Bombay had forty-four Parsi prostitutes, according to the census of 1864," Karela said, working his way through his index of trivia.

We exited the libertine troposphere of Falkland Road and walked towards Tardeo. The plan was to eat chaat at Swati Snacks, where terrific food was served efficiently in the clinical glow of tubelight reflecting off steel surfaces. As we walked, I filled Karela in on my conversations with Burjor's friends. He listened attentively, looking in my direction while stroking his limp goatee, another sign he was long unused to the more crowded, anarchic parts of the city. He stumbled on the chipped pavement, tunnelled into pedestrians, received abuses—watch where you walk, motherfucker—till I told him, "For god's sake, stop walking like you're the only one on this road. Look ahead!"

"Now that you know all this about Burjor, how do you feel?"

"I'm not sure. My father had an impressive mercantile brain but no scruples when it came to women."

"All great men are assholes in some way."

"Would you call him a great man?"

"The employment bureau was a stroke of genius, an

example of ballsy Parsi entrepreneurship that's entirely lacking today."

"I don't know. It seems such a mercenary thing to do. Why did he take money from those poor people? He was earning enough selling booze and contraband."

"This is your privilege speaking. He came from nothing, which meant he had to make a living every way he could. He couldn't afford to be apologetic about money."

We hailed a cab. Karela was walking dangerously, barrelling through commuters who'd exited the station on the narrow pavement. He couldn't be trusted to make it to Swati without causing a casualty or becoming one. I wanted no delay for the image of dahi batata puri was dancing in my mind.

"Let's face it, he was a crook," I said.

"What do you think businessmen are if not crooks? You don't make money without fucking people over or scamming the system. Parsis made fortunes selling opium at the cost of the Chinese, remember. Do I have to teach you how capital works at this advanced age?"

Since it was well past lunchtime, there was no queue outside Swati Snacks. We rushed in and I ordered for both of us—dahi batata puri, panki chutney and rava dosa.

"What about the other great Parsi virtue of philanthropy? If he did this pro bono, he could've been a businessman and a benefactor. The great smugglers of Bombay were very charitable. Haji Mastan showered money on the poor, championed the rights of dalits and Muslims."

"You're missing the point entirely."

"Bear with me, I'm playing devil's advocate here. You don't think he profited from fifty-fifties when he didn't need to?"

"What makes you think he didn't need to? He wasn't a big-league smuggler. He left you a Ricoh, not a Rolex."

Our food arrived. Steaming dosa and panki that we scraped off banana leaves and dipped in a pungent chutney. Puris plump with potato and mung, overflowing with curd and chutneys, crowned with sev of the correct thickness. Not the fat variety that lodged itself in your teeth and not the skinny type that lacked crunch either. We ate for a few minutes in silence.

"Look at Homi," Karela continued. "You said he continued in the smuggling business after Burjor left. If he'd made enough he would've been set up for life. He wouldn't need his low-paying admin job."

"Who knows, maybe he has a stash of gold somewhere."

"You're forgetting Burjor's unique circumstances," Karela went on. "At that time, upward mobility was rare for people like him. Plus, he had a stepmother determined to avenge herself for her husband's misdemeanour by making Burjor a servant. He helped himself splendidly. And others, in an imaginative, audacious way. Don't forget he was living in a colony, a conservative place full of rednecks who hate the idea of Parsis mingling with outsiders."

"He could've done more to help Armaity."

"As I said, genius goes hand in hand with bad behaviour. Borges was sympathetic to Pinochet. Picasso was a sleaze. Nicola Tesla believed in eugenics. Einstein was a terrible husband."

"I worry I've inherited Burjor's attitude when it comes to the opposite sex."

"What do you mean?"

"He was disingenuous in love. He was averse to commitment, yet he projected the illusion that he was truly into the woman he was seeing or bonking at a time. As soon as she began making the predictable noises of wanting more from the relationship, he backed off. It's perhaps the only cliché that can be attached to him."

We were on dessert, hand-churned ice cream. Karela was practically inhaling his scoop of roasted almond. I was trying out the coffee orange.

"So you're a commitment-phobe, what's the big deal? Frankly you need to worry more about making something of yourself. How's the writing coming along? The magazine article and the chapter you owe me. You were too scared to find Burjor while he was still alive. Don't let your bullshit anxieties stop you from telling his story."

"Jesus, you're not my teacher anymore."

"By the way, I happened to speak to Jamshed. The editor of his site is going to call you with an offer for the job."

31

The death of Armaity had the effect of quelling the paranoia Phiroze had whipped up against Burjor among a section of the colony. This meant he could walk around the place without being buffeted by malignant stares. Though in those days, Burjor was too tied up to really notice, having to hold the reigns of his various businesses from Naval Baug even as he babysat and ran the home.

The three women took turns to feed, clean and play with me and put me to sleep. Each would sing. Jermai sang Gujarati songs as she walked around the house, thumping my infant back with her arthritic fists. She would spend her last days bent at odd angles like a contortionist frozen mid-pose, divine comeuppance, according to Hilla, for her scheming ways. Hilla crooned Frank Sinatra tunes, 'My Funny Valentine', 'I've Got You Under My Skin'. Imelda softly sang hymns into my drowsy ears. Perhaps that's why even a sceptic like me is moved at the sight of people in prayer. Mini would take me to Holy Name Cathedral in Colaba every Christmas, where, on seeing clasped hands and bowed heads and listening to the hymnal chorus, a lump would materialize in my throat.

—

Had Burjor had the capacity to tune into the life of the colony, he might have heard the few shrill voices against him that refused to pipe down. He might have seen suspicious conferences between people, some of whom openly hated him. It was good for them Burjor didn't notice. They were such amateurs, they didn't even think of concealing themselves while plotting. If there's one thing I'd learned after editing all those crime stories is that most people don't have a clue when it comes to serious crime. You're a suspected killer on the run. You turn on your mobile phone to make a call, the next thing you know the cops are at your door. You kidnap a kid, make a ransom demand and show up to collect the cash thinking the parents would've sincerely listened to your threat and not called the cops. Or you murder someone, stick the body in a suitcase covered with your DNA and abandon it near the mangroves, where it's found days later by fisherfolk or couples looking for a spot to canoodle.

Usually, Burjor was loath to leave me alone with Jermai. But on days Imelda was busy and he had to leave the colony for work, he had no choice.

Burjor came home one such evening to find Jermai hysterical, her hair a mess, her blouse half out of the waistband of her skirt. The floor was scattered with newspapers, a chair had been upturned, the linen on the bed had been messed up. Beating her chest like an orangutan, Jermai told Burjor that masked men had entered the apartment and spirited me away. She'd put up a dogged fight but how could an infirm, old woman like her match two hulking men? Before leaving, they had told her to tell Burjor that they would be in touch.

"Why the need for this set-up? If the kidnappers were looking for something, I'd understand the papers on the floor, etcetera. But they were only interested in the baby," I said. "I was the centre of a crime carried out by a couple of blundering shmucks. Burjor must have seen through it immediately."

"Not immediately, but it didn't take too long for the whole plan to collapse," Jimmy said. "He wasn't in the frame of mind for forensic analysis. He panicked, we were all up in arms. Where's Moonie? Who took Moonie?"

Burjor summoned Homi, who was at his usual table in a bar in Mazagaon. And then went over to Hilla and Jimmy's with Jermai in tow. In between cinematic sobs, she repeated the story.

"We thought the culprits must be Burjor's enemies or something," Hilla said. "It was natural to assume, given his line of work."

But Burjor didn't have the kind of enemies who'd go so far as to kidnap his child. The only grand rivalry he had was with Phiroze. It must be him! Phiroze had been out to get him for years, there could be no one else.

"I wasn't convinced," Jimmy said. "Phiroze had been hanging out in the compound that day as usual with his gang. If he was guilty, he wouldn't have been able to hide it. Trust me, you couldn't expect subtlety from the guy."

Burjor, however, became convinced Phiroze had kidnapped me. Rushing out of the house with dissenting Jimmy and Hilla and an encouraging Jermai in tow, Burjor made for Phiroze's. The guy lived with his parents and, at the time, they were having dinner. Phiroze opened the door with a mouthful of cutlet, nearly choking when Burjor grabbed him by the throat. Phiroze's father, a fighter in the same mould as his son, leapt up and tried to wrestle Burjor. Poor Jimmy, who had (and still has) the slim frame of a dancer and who abhorred violence, felt compelled to enter the tripartite fray for the sake of his friend. He tried to prise Phiroze's father from Burjor and got knocked against the wall. The commotion drew people to the balconies. Another bust-up between Phiroze and Burjor! Here was a more delicious dessert than caramel custard. After a few minutes of scuffle, it became clear that Phiroze was not the kidnapper. Go to the police bhenchod, instead of wasting time, Phiroze yelled.

"Obviously we did not want to go to the police," Homi said. It was the year of the Emergency. The cops had been coming down hard on smugglers for months and Burjor had already been raided.

Burjor dispatched Homi to gather intelligence from their network of smugglers and petty criminals on who could bear such a heavy grudge. Hilla and Jimmy went home after Burjor assured them he would go to the cops the following day if nothing turned up. And Burjor returned to his flat to await a ransom call and to interrogate Jermai one more time.

Two men had rung the bell, she'd opened the door innocently, Jermai said. Why would she bother to be careful in this safe enclave of god-fearing Parsis? One of them, a moustachioed fellow who looked like a "Madrasi villain" clamped a hand over her mouth and held her tight as she tried to wrench free. The other went into the room and picked up the sleeping baby. Before leaving, they barked that Burjor could expect to hear from them and pressed a moist handkerchief against her nose. She passed out briefly and on coming to, immediately went over to Jimmy and Hilla's.

"Earlier, you'd said they were masked," Burjor said.

Jermai froze as she recalled the earlier version of the story, her brain scrambled to concoct a cover-up. But she went blank as Burjor (in my imagination) moved towards her, a menacing leviathan. At that moment, when the old crone was certain Burjor was about to crack her gnarled limbs, the bell rang. Phiroze was at the door with Hilla and Jimmy and me, a gurgling bundle, in his arms.

"Phiroze!" I said.

"Finding you was probably the only decent thing that man has done in his life," Hilla said.

Burjor's first reaction was to lunge for Phiroze's throat. Phiroze had anticipated this which is why he'd brought Hilla and Jimmy along. As soon as Burjor moved, the couple restrained him. Once again, delicate Jimmy was forced to pit his feeble strength against Burjor.

"It was like trying to control a rabid dog," Jimmy said. "If Hilla wasn't there, Burjor would have finished me and Phiroze."

Unlike Burjor, whose work outside Naval Baug removed him from the interactions, relationships, the movements that made up the rich matrix of life in the colony, Phiroze was always tuned in. Since he did practically nothing, both his feet were firmly planted in the bed of the colony's life-stream. There was nothing that occurred in the place that didn't wash through him. So Phiroze had heard the trill of voices against Burjor and seen the suspicious conferences from his panoptic perch, the balcony outside his home. So he knew exactly where to go.

When Boman opened the door for Phiroze that night, Phiroze looked past the old man and saw me, serenely playing with my rattle on a nest of swaddling clothes on the couch. The same rattle, I presume, that arrived with the rest of the objects in the box.

Estranged from his son Cyrus, Burjor's one-time rival, Boman had racked up gambling debts and a substantial booze bill that he couldn't pay. The country liquor bar near the colony refused him credit till he paid up. Sober and more irascible than usual, Boman stood on the balcony and railed against Burjor and the world.

"He was a nuisance, especially on weekends," said Jimmy, who lived one floor below Boman. "You'd be trying to read the papers on Sunday. Suddenly Boman would start and his soliloquy would reach us like the voice of god."

Phiroze had also seen Boman and Jermai's animated discussions, a suspicious activity since, while they knew each other having lived in the same place for decades, they could hardly be called friends. The two of them prepared a scheme to kidnap me and ransom Burjor. Boman needed the cash to clear his debt so he could drink again and Jermai would do anything for a reward. Boman weighed the plan with a moral imperative—Burjor needed to be taught a lesson for vitiating the blood-bound Zoroastrian identity. As if Jermai needed any more convincing.

On the day Burjor was forced to leave me alone with Jermai, the crone bundled my sleeping form into a large shopping bag and walked across to Boman's flat. It was late afternoon on a working day, which meant that folks were either away or indoors. No one seeing Jermai's bow-legged crawl across the quadrangle would've been suspicious since she was often seen walking around with the bag. Usually, it was filled with parcels of leftover food from people's homes.

"Are you saying I was silent throughout the journey,

that I didn't wake up, start bawling and bring people to the balconies?" I said.

"You were not a cry-baby," Hilla said.

"Still, it's hard to imagine an infant keeping quiet inside a stinking shopping bag."

"You were drugged, I'm willing to bet," Imelda said. "She must have given you a lick of opium. A man like this Boman character would have known how to get it."

After depositing me with Boman, Jermai returned to the apartment and clumsily staged the mise en scène of a break-in.

"The stupid old woman was doing whatever came into her head," Jimmy said. "And what came into her head was what she had seen in movies."

"Phiroze hated Burjor. How come he rescued me?"

"I guess what Boman did was too despicable even for a blackguard like Phiroze," Jimmy said.

When the plot unravelled, Jermai exploded into a theatrical plea for mercy. She was dispatched to her home and told to stay put till Burjor figured what had to be done. The series of events that followed is unclear, understandably so for Burjor was reluctant to reveal too much. That night Burjor visited Boman. Did the two have loud words? No one in the colony heard a fight. But there was a scuffle and three days later, Boman was found dead in his bathroom.

As Boman's body atrophied, Burjor flew around Bombay organizing his flight. He told the truth to Homi and Imelda since they had the stomach for shady stuff, that he had delivered Boman a blow that was likely to be fatal. The man was barely alive when Burjor left him. But he told Jimmy and Hilla, without offering any details, that he'd "straightened out" Boman.

"He was protecting us," Jimmy said.

"And himself," Hilla said. "He knew you'd go to the police. You're too upright."

"As if you would have kept mum. He killed a man Hilla."

"Not intentionally. I don't think I would've gone to the police."

"He killed a man! You're saying this now, after years have blunted the seriousness of his actions. If you'd known then, you would've been scared the cops would think you're an accomplice."

"Thank Jesus he didn't tell these two," Imelda said.

Over two days, Burjor met Mini, who, fortunately for him and me, was in an emotionally amenable frame of mind. He sold the cab and handed over the employment businesses and what was left of the smuggling racket to Homi. Imelda wrote Burjor's parting missive. Then he made his way to Nepal, never to return. Three days later, Boman's body was found. Overcome with curiosity—she hadn't seen Boman on her daily perambulations—to the point of being heedless of Burjor's threat to decapitate her should she be seen with the old villain, Jermai, under the cover of night (though there's only so much stealth a slow-moving, arthritic woman can muster), rang his bell. She returned the next day, emboldened by

Burjor's absence. When there was no answer, she alerted his neighbours. Phiroze, whose ears were perpetually glued to the colony's substratum, materialized almost immediately. He barrelled his shoulder into Boman's door and when it finally gave, he and Jermai were hit with the miasma of mortified flesh.

"After that, everything came out," Hilla said. "It was a scandal. People still talk about it. Jermai was totally exposed."

"I felt sorry for her though," Jimmy said. "People stopped giving her food, stopped getting her to deliver milk. Good thing she didn't live too long."

The old devil should have had a death as tragic as Boman's for all the crimes she'd committed. Yet, she passed in her sleep. No one noticed till the smell of her decaying body reached the other widows in the building. She should've gone to jail. Instead, Homi spent weeks in the slammer, getting beaten by cops wanting to know Burjor's whereabouts. It would've been easy to trace Burjor's movements to Mini's door. But the police lost interest. The Emergency was underway. They didn't have the time to chase a petty smuggler, who'd knocked off a no-good drunk with a gambling addiction.

"Did Burjor plan to return?" I said.

"We didn't discuss it but I have my doubts, Moonie," Homi said.

32

After lunch at Swati Snacks, Karela and I walked up Forjett Street and took a left towards Nana Chowk, sharing a joint as we strolled. The idea was to work off some of the lunch. On the way, we passed Hormaz Watch Company, an old watch repair shop that, I could see through the glass door, was packed with antique clocks. I returned the following day to the shop to get Burjor's Ricoh fixed, filled with sentimental desire to wear a sign of the guy. But after being fixed, the watch would fog up with the slightest moisture. The sweat from my wrist was enough to cause a beady film of condensation, obscuring the dial.

"Don't bother with that. You couldn't count on him for anything," Mini said, as usual speaking of Burjor with a degree of familiarity greater than the actual weight of their relationship.

We were in my room; Mini was absorbing the coda of Burjor's saga. After years of being her confidante, I could accurately divine her thoughts. She was experiencing a moment of intense unreality, of horror that she, the daughter of cultured Leftists from Bengal, who could quote from Shakespeare's tragedies (she hates the comedies), who taught literature at a college, could fall for someone capable of base actions. How could she have dreamt of a life with a taxi driver, a person belonging to a class of people whose dreadful lives breed violent tendencies? The feeling was intensified by the newly sprung geyser of warmth between her and Shivaji that cast a mist over the past, softening its ugliness.

"No one will think you were born to Leftists hearing you talk," I said. "What happened to wanting a classless society? The truth is that you were depressed at that time in your life. If that rhino who lives on the first floor had showed you affection, you'd have fallen for him. Also, let's not forget your spectacular naivete when it comes to men. You thought you had it good with Shivaji, a chubby brat who had even less in common with you than Burjor. At least with Burjor, you could explore the city, eat steak."

"Things are good between your father and me now."

"It took thirty-five years and a brush with death."

"Say what you like about Shivaji, but he didn't walk away from responsibility. Your Burjor didn't call even once all the time he was away. Now don't say he was a fugitive, obviously he couldn't call. You think the cops had nothing better to do than to keep tabs on the death of a gambler and drunkard?"

I was edgy that morning. The following day was to be my first at the new job. The thought of working in the intangible, unfamiliar digital sphere, where speed is paramount and there's little time for reflection, had my stomach in knots. So much so that I'd taken a shit thrice before noon. Even more unsettling was the thought of being in close proximity to dishy Jamshed Shroff. Hopefully the infatuation would soon pass. But till then, I'd suffer wicked visions silently as Jamshed either carried on oblivious or ignored my pitiful signals. Feeling restless, I stepped out for a solitary jaunt.

—

No matter how genteel it got, Arthur Bunder Road never lost its whisper of vice. Every year a new gallery or boutique opened in the street's two massive buildings, that had once been warehouses of cotton waiting to be shipped to England and later a den of shady businesses. Yet, the ghosts of brothels past hung like an out-of-reach cobweb over the stretch. As I turned left on to Apollo Bunder, the voice of my inner tour guide clicked on.

This stretch of buildings came up around the twenties and thirties, just before art deco took the city by storm. Each building is different. The first one is Shelleys Hotel. The well-known astrologer BJ has lived here for nearly a decade. It used to be Lentin Court, after the owner Phirozeshaw Lentin. Back then, these buildings were occupied mostly by Europeans and westernized Indians: Parsis, Gujaratis, Muslims. The apartments were modern. For instance, they had attached bathrooms, a novel feature at the time.

I walked towards the Taj, running my hand along the stone seawall smooth from contact with millions of bodies. My adamantine support, and the combined stone of the veteran buildings, the Taj to the left, the Gateway to the right and Yacht Club ahead, had the desired effect, settling the quivering muscles of my agitated belly. Since the place was crowded with tourists, I decided to continue my ramble in Ballard Estate. And there in front of me, as if placed by an omniscient hand, was a taxi with a sticker of an asho farohar, the Zoroastrian winged divinity, indicating that either the driver or owner was Parsi.

Of course, I got in. An archetypal face, tanned but fair, black wings for eyebrows, a hook of a nose, skinny lips, turned towards me.

"Madam, just one minute, if you don't mind," said the young face.

"Sure."

He turned to his phone and finished watching the remaining minute of a dance video. Looking over his shoulder, I could tell it was a contemporary performance with dancers in nude body suits making anarchic movements. Involuntarily, I held my breath, experiencing the potent sensation of being at the threshold of a great story. A Parsi taxi driver in this day was a freak occurrence but one intensely interested in contemporary dance...what gift was chance serving me?

"Sorry madam," he said sheepishly, keeping his phone aside. "Where you want to go?"

"Ballard Estate...you like dance?"

His name was Kaizad Bharucha. He was nineteen and lived in a colony in Bombay Central. Normally, his father drove the cab but the old man had been ill for months forcing Kaizad to take over. The arrangement had temporarily put on hold Kaizad's dancing career. He was a trained Bharatanatyam dancer.

"I have done lots and lots of shows, in Mumbai and outside also," he said.

"How the hell does a Parsi boy living in a colony learn Bharatanatyam?" I said.

A woman in his colony ran a dance school. She was a fan of the legendary Vajifdar sisters, Shirin, Roshan and Khurshid, who in the thirties and forties appalled conservative Parsis by dancing in public. Shirin, who was considered one of the brilliant dancers of her age, mastered Kathakali, Bharatanatyam and Manipuri. Kaizad's parents had signed him up at a young age thinking he'd be better off learning a discipline than spending his free time just hanging out in the colony. At a red light, Kaizad showed me pictures of himself in Bharatanatyam livery. Was it the charge of finding a terrific story or my vigorous hormones for there was something erotic about Kaizad's pale, athletic torso with a slim column of hair between his pecs like a line of coke, all of it emerging from a red and yellow silk dhoti. The kid was nineteen! I had to remind myself.

Two years ago, a classmate had shown him videos of Martha Graham and Pina Bausch and introduced him to a famous choreographer in the city who had a dance studio. Kaizad began training at the studio by paying a subsidized fee. But that had stopped when his father fell ill. At the next signal, he showed me a video of a group performance. Wearing loose satin pajamas, Kaizad leapt, whirled and sinuously manoeuvred his body in gravity-defying ways. The dancers coalesced, fitting the joints of their bodies together till they resembled an organism. Then they began to furl and unfurl. Beneath his loose cabbie's uniform was a rippling body. I looked up and noticed the ropy heft of his forearms on the steering wheel. He's nineteen! I had to tell myself again.

"What does it look like?" Kaizad said.

"Umm...a pulsing vagina?" I muttered.

"What?"

"No, I don't know. You tell me."

"A flower."

"Fucking fantastic," I said. "You should be training in London or Germany. Your future is in Europe or America, not here."

"Ya, I want to. I've applied to one Parsi trust for funds. But I don't know. Lot of applicants are there. There are people who want to be lawyers and engineers and all. Don't know whether they'll give to a dancer."

I was going into my new job with a crackling story. Kaizad agreed to let me interview him, his family and teachers and follow him around. A story like his was bound to get press, perhaps the attention of benefactors. I made up my mind to speak to my old adversary

Mahrukh, who could push his case at some trust. We pulled up near the World War I memorial at Ballard Estate and exchanged numbers.

"Madam, thank you for helping me," Kaizad said.

You don't know this but you're really helping me, I thought as I walked into the serene, stony grid of Ballard Estate.

This here on the right is the Ballard Bunder Gatehouse, which was built in 1920 to commemorate Ballard Pier. It houses a little naval museum now. If you go inside, you'll see a modest but lovely collection of photographs of the area and naval models. The gate was once the entrance to the Ballard Pier railway station. As the name suggests, this was once a pier. So you could get off the ship from England and then get on to the Frontier Mail...

EPILOGUE

My profile of Kaizad, 'the pirouetting Parsi' (I wasn't above alliteration, either) went viral. Soon after it was published, journalists besieged him, including Tumpa, who wanted to write a piece for her foreign publication. A filmmaker looking for inspiring stories wanted to make a short documentary on Kaizad. I didn't have to call Mahrukh. A major trust got in touch with him and offered a full scholarship to the dance school he was keen on. The last time we met was at a celebratory tea party at his home. His overcome parents, marvelling at my Parsi looks, served me tea with mint and lemongrass, mava cake and mutton cutlets. Kaizad, wearing shorts and a sadra whose gossamer material barely veiled his sinewy shape, amused me by communicating with his eyes and hands, the Bharatanatyam dancer's dumb charades.

After working on it for nearly twenty years, Karela finally published his mischievous anthology, *The Parsi Pirate: Stories of Rebels and Unsung Heroes*. In keeping with the roguish nature of his subjects, Karela released the book in a dive in Grant Road East, not far from Kamathipura, the red light district we'd visited together. The place used to be a dance bar back when dance bars were legal, and the book had a chapter on the owner. Karela was in high spirits, channelling his teacher's voice while talking to journalists, laughing ostentatiously.

Karela had persuaded me to read from the chapter I'd written on Burjor, 'Burjor Elavia: The Full Life of a Fifty-fifty'. (The curse of the alliteration!) In the audience were more journalists than I'd expected. Karela's friends, including a couple of teachers from school, who, unsurprisingly, had no recollection of me, Homi, Imelda, Hilla and Jimmy, who beamed proudly in the first row. Altaf Arsiwala, now Homi's landlord, had arrived, the painful grind and scrape of his arthritic joints forgotten in the excitement of an outing, an event in an unseemly part of town with the press in attendance. What a story he had to tell his kids on the weekly telephone conversations in which they dully participated. Mini had come with Shivaji. She hadn't wanted to bring him along fearing an emotional meltdown brought on by the experience of hearing me talk about Burjor. That's exactly what happened. Halfway through the reading as I looked up to scan the audience, I saw Mini with her handkerchief stuffed in her mouth, her face wet and swollen like a ripe plum. Next to her, Shivaji shifted bashfully in his seat. In the old dispensation, she would've come without him. But in their new, loving order of things, Mini and

Shivaji did everything together. As I looked beyond the purple bulb of Mini's head, I met the gaze that I felt most keenly, that of Jamshed, who sat in a corner in a penumbra of pricey cologne.

What did I feel airing my word-picture of Burjor, committing his form, for so long shaped inside my mind, to the public sphere? Like I was delivering a portrait that had been in the works for an age. Yet, after all that time, the image that emerged was essentially mysterious, a teasing flash built of the shifting memories that remained in the mind's subtle matter. But it was enough to produce a fleeting moment more precious than the Ricoh watch, the boy's sadra, the mother-of-pearl broach or anything in Burjor's cardboard bequest... the sense of having created meaning. At the end of the reading, someone in the audience asked whether after everything I knew about Burjor, I thought he was a good man.

"Well, half of him was at any rate," I said.

ACKNOWLEDGEMENTS

I'm enormously grateful to Kaevan Umrigar and Rusheed Wadia for their generosity in helping me with my research; Rati, for telling me the story that started me off on this project; Amit Gurbaxani, for patiently reading my early drafts and offering encouragement; Sarosh, for his support and constant entertainment; and my editor Aruna Ghose for her thoughtful critique and for pushing my story in exciting directions.